SLOW PATH TO PEACE

A MATURE-AGE CHRISTIAN ROMANCE

JULIETTE DUNCAN

A SUNBURNED LAND - BOOK 3

Cover Design by http://www.StunningBookCovers.com

Copyright © 2020 Juliette Duncan

All rights reserved.

SLOW PATH TO PEACE is a work of fiction. Names, characters, and incidents are all products of the author's imagination or are used for fictional purposes. Any mentioned brand names, places, and trade marks remain the property of their respective owners, bear no association with the author, and are used for fictional purposes only.

THE HOLY BIBLE, NEW INTERNATIONAL VERSION®, NIV® Copyright © 1973, 1978, 1984, 2011 by Biblica, Inc.™ Used by permission. All rights reserved worldwide.

PRAISE FOR "SLOW PATH TO PEACE"

"I was eagerly awaiting this book. Having read the first two in the series I was keen to find out what happened to Serena and David. I was not disappointed. This story had me gripped from start to finish." *~Judith*

"I really enjoyed this faith filled story. I enjoyed how the family members have grown & cried when 2 new believer's came to faith. I know this story is not true but it brings to mind when other's truly come to be believer's & take that exciting path. I liked that this book brought out how bad circumstances can bring us to Christ even though He doesn't cause them He uses them for good. Truly our God is a wondrous God & brings this out in real stories. " *~Patricia*

"Another heartfelt win for this series! I've always loved Australia and to continue to read stories taken place in this beautiful part of the country always warms my soul. A story that continues the love in families that grew to be our friends and seeing how God continues to move in their lives. Such amazing grace! " *~Sharon D.*

FOREWORD

HELLO! Thank you for choosing to read this book - I hope you enjoy it! Please note that this story is set in Australia. Australian spelling and terminology have been used and are not typos!

As a thank you for reading this book, I'd like to offer you a FREE GIFT. That's right - my FREE novella, "Hank and Sarah - A Love Story" is available exclusively to my newsletter subscribers. Click here to claim your copy now and to be notified of my future book releases. I hope you enjoy both books! Have a wonderful day!

Juliette

CHAPTER 1

Returning to Goddard Downs after their two-week honeymoon was like coming back to earth with a thud. How Maggie wished she and Frank could have stayed forever in the idyllic seaside town of Broome where the troubles they'd left behind had faded a little with each passing day as the two of them had fallen further and further in love.

But now, as the small plane descended towards Kununurra airport, Maggie wondered what awaited them. Her daughter Serena was very much on her heart and mind, and while she'd prayed every day for her, Maggie didn't know whether she was still at Goddard Downs, or whether she'd returned to Darwin. Maggie had also prayed daily for David, Serena's ex-partner, and that their unexpected breakup the night before Maggie and Frank's wedding hadn't sent him into a tailspin.

Cliff, Maggie's ex-husband, also weighed heavily on her mind. Before she and Frank left for their honeymoon, she'd gathered something was afoot with him but didn't pursue it.

She hadn't wanted to. But now, she couldn't help but think of him. Jeremy, her adult son who lived in Darwin, had promised to look out for both Cliff and David, but that was a huge responsibility when he had two small children of his own to care for.

She also wondered how the plans for the tourism venture were coming along. Would the overnight cattle drives and the eco tents be enough to save Goddard Downs following the ban on live cattle exports? She and Frank had purposefully avoided talking about these matters while on their honeymoon after committing them all to God, but now they would be facing them afresh.

She also knew that handing over the reins of Goddard Downs to Julian, his eldest son, was causing Frank some anxiety. He'd said he was happy to take a step back, but Maggie sensed he wasn't completely ready.

Leaning across her, he glanced out the window before grinning and stealing a kiss. "Are you ready to go home, my love?" As he searched her eyes, her insides went to jelly like they always did whenever he looked at her with his pale blue eyes she could lose herself in forever.

She gave a small smile and shifted in the seat, tearing her gaze from his to stare out the window. For the last forty years or more, home for her had been Darwin, Australia's northernmost city. Her new home was Goddard Downs, the cattle station that had been in Frank's family for four generations and was more than a thousand kilometres from Darwin. It was remote and almost totally inaccessible by road during the wet season. Their nearest neighbours were several hours' drive away. Their main means of transport during the wet season was helicopter, although they could catch a ride on the mail plane once a week if there was room, or head up to the tiny port town of Wyndham via a backroad if they were desperate. They stockpiled supplies during the dry season because running out during the wet season was not only inconvenient but expensive. They slaughtered their own beef, pigs and poultry, so there was always plenty of meat, and they grew most of their own vegetables. She'd stayed there for six weeks as a guest prior to their wedding, but now she was arriving as the wife of the owner. *Was she ready?*

She swung her gaze back to his and looked into the eyes she'd come to know and love. Eyes that were clear, honest, and trustworthy. *Was she ready?*

Other than one incident with Julian, she'd felt loved and accepted by the family, but would anything change now that she was married to the current patriarch?

She had no intention of taking over the running of the homestead. She and Frank would live in the log cabin beside the lagoon, half a kilometre away. Janella, Julian's wife, and Olivia, Frank's daughter, were both capable young women and she wouldn't dare intrude unless invited.

There was nothing to worry about, and yet, a small sense of unease filled her. But there was no need to concern Frank. It was simply insecurity from her days married to Cliff rearing its head.

She recalled the passage from Colossians chapter three that Olivia read at their wedding. *Therefore, as God's chosen people, holy and dearly loved, clothe yourselves with compassion, kindness, humility, gentleness and patience. Bear with each other and forgive one another if any of you has a grievance against someone. Forgive as the Lord forgave you. And over all these virtues put on love, which binds them all together in perfect unity.* That would be her mantra going forward. She would clothe herself with compassion and kindness, she would be humble and gentle, and she would love Frank's family as her own. Because that's what they were now—her family.

She smiled at him and simply replied, "Yes."

CHAPTER 2

*J*ulian greeted them at the airport, and after hugs and kisses, Maggie and Frank collected their bags and hurried to the helicopter pad where the Goddard Downs helicopter awaited them. It was mid-afternoon and a large bank of menacing clouds was rapidly approaching from the east.

"I hope we can outfly that, son," Frank said. "Do you think we should wait until it passes?"

Julian frowned. "Where've you been, Dad? That's not going to pass. It's the low from Cyclone Lilly coming our way."

"Oh. I didn't know. We'd better hurry."

Maggie listened to the exchange between the two and tried not to grow concerned as she clambered inside the helicopter. Frank ushered her into the front seat beside Julian then he jumped in the back. She wasn't sure where she'd rather be—up front where she could see the storm clouds brewing, or in the back where she could close her eyes and zone out, but it was too late to choose. Julian had started the engine and was awaiting instructions. She figured they wouldn't be allowed to take off if it was deemed unsafe, and that gave her a level of comfort, but the menacing clouds loomed closer every second. They'd be flying away from them, but she doubted they'd be airborne before the rain started.

She was right. Moments later, heavy drops sploshed on the windscreen, and within seconds, the rain was so heavy she could barely see the terminal. The noise was deafening. Neither Julian nor Frank seemed perturbed, or if they were, they hid it well. Julian received the all clear and prepared for take-off, and within moments, the helicopter was airborne. Frozen in her seat, Maggie held her breath. She'd flown in helicopters and small planes before, but never in bad weather. She trusted Julian, but her heart pounded. In an attempt to calm it, she took some deep breaths and prayed. It was all she could do.

The wind buffeted the helicopter and for a moment she thought they were going down, but then it broke through the clouds into glorious sunshine and relief flowed through her veins. She breathed easy and her body relaxed.

The flight to Goddard Downs was a short one—less than half an hour, but the landscape below was breathtaking. Red and ochre ancient rock formations, and dark, jagged outlines of ridges and plateaus framed the vast savannah plains. It was rugged country, but it was beautiful. The Ord River had burst its banks and the low-lying land now looked like an inland sea.

Goddard Downs came into view. Sprawled over one-hundred-and-fifty-thousand acres, the station was huge and spread further than the eye could see, but it wasn't as huge as some. Nearby Bullo River Station was over five-hundred-thousand acres.

This was now her home. Although Maggie had been raised on a station, it had been much smaller and not nearly so remote. She wondered briefly what the years ahead would bring. She and Frank had vowed to love and cherish each other in sickness and in health, for richer or poorer, until death did they part. Neither was young, but God willing, they had plenty of years left to enjoy together. But no one knew what lay in their future—only God was privy to that information. Whatever lay ahead, He would be with them and would uphold and sustain them, because that was His promise to His children.

The homestead came into view, drawing Maggie from her reverie. Frank must have sensed her anxiety when Julian steered the helicopter towards the pad because he reached forward and gave her shoulder a squeeze. She lifted a hand and placed it over his, drawing comfort.

The helicopter descended and came to a stop, and as the whirring subsided, she turned around and briefly caught his gaze. Julian jumped out and Frank did likewise, offering his hand to help her down. Being short made anything like this difficult, but she didn't mind, especially when Frank caught her in his arms and kissed her before setting her safely on the ground.

Julian strode to the shed and returned with a quad bike. He and Frank transferred their luggage from the helicopter to the bike, and then they all climbed in. Maggie once again sat in the front beside Julian for the short ride.

"The girls are preparing a welcome home dinner," he said as he steered the quad in the direction of the cabin.

"That's nice of them," Maggie said, smiling. "What time are we expected?"

"About six. That should give you enough time to freshen up."

"That's more than enough time. Is…is Serena still here?" She tried not to allow her anxiety to show in her voice.

Julian faced her, his expression blank, and Maggie wondered if there was a problem. "Yes, but she's been looking forward to you coming back."

Maggie studied him carefully, trying to read between the lines. Something seemed afoot but she wasn't sure what. She smiled and turned her gaze to the front. Whatever it was, she'd find out shortly.

With Serena and David broken up, Maggie expected she'd take over the role of Serena's main carer but was unsure how that would work with her being newly married. Frank would understand, of course, but it could place a strain on their relationship. She prayed it wouldn't and trusted God to figure it out.

When Julian pulled up outside the cabin, Maggie had a flashback of her first visit to Goddard Downs less than a year ago, and how gobsmacked she'd been when Olivia had brought her down here. She'd expected a simple cabin with basic facilities, not this gorgeous log cabin with a wraparound verandah and a clear view to the lagoon. How many times since then had she sat on one of the rockers, simply enjoying the view while she was meant to be working? She imagined that she and Frank would make full use of the rockers in the days and weeks to come.

Frank jumped down and extended his hand to her, a broad

grin on his face. She took his hand and carefully climbed out. Julian had already placed their luggage on the verandah and was back in the driver's seat. "See you tonight." He tipped his hat and sped off.

Left alone, Frank slipped his arms around her and lowered his mouth towards hers. "Home, sweet home," he whispered between kisses.

Laughing, she kissed him back. She would never get enough of Frank Goddard. How blessed she was to have him as her husband, especially after her disastrous marriage to Cliff.

Taking her by surprise, Frank swept her into his arms and carried her up the stairs like a man half his sixty-two years. "Frank! What are you doing?"

"Carrying you over the threshold, that's what I'm doing."

She laughed again before he set her down on the highly polished timber floor. Their gazes met and held, and for a moment, time stood still. Her heart beat faster as he closed the gap between them and enveloped her in his arms. Arms that made her feel safe, secure, loved. She tipped her head and gazed into his eyes. "I love you, Frank."

"And I love you right back." Lowering his mouth, he brushed his lips gently across hers. "How much time have we got?"

She chuckled. "Not enough for what you're thinking."

His bottom lip protruded in a pout. "I guess we'll have to wait until later."

"Yes. We can't be late for dinner." Planting a kiss on his lips, she ducked under his arms and grinned. "Dibs on first shower."

"From memory, I think it's big enough for two."

"Frank! Behave!"

His shoulders drooped. "All right. If I must."

"You must." She chuckled and then looked around. "Why don't you make yourself useful and grab our bags?"

"Oh, right. I'd forgotten about them."

"I thought so." She shook her head and laughed.

Once the bags were inside, Maggie followed Frank up the stairs to the master suite, a loft-like room that took up the entire floor. With windows on every side, it offered a panoramic view that Maggie would never tire of. She loved waking up in the king-sized bed overlooking the lagoon. Now she'd love it more because she'd be waking with Frank beside her.

"I think I'll take a bath," she said, walking over to the west facing window and gazing out.

"Well, I know for a fact that bath's big enough for two," Frank said, setting the bags down. His father had spared no expense when he built the cabin for his bride many years earlier, and it had taken six men to haul the giant porcelain claw-foot tub through the window.

"You don't give up easily, do you?" Turning, she slipped her arms around his waist and lifted her palm to his cheek. "We'll have plenty of time later, okay?"

He smiled and covered her hand with his before gently kissing her palm. "I guess I'll have to be happy with that."

"Good. Now, we run the risk of being late for dinner, so on second thought, I'll take a shower and save the bath for another day."

CHAPTER 3

Instead of taking the quad bike that had been left for them outside the cabin, Frank and Maggie decided to walk the short distance to the homestead for their welcome home dinner. The rain they'd flown through in Kununurra hadn't reached Goddard Downs, and the sky was a deep, gorgeous blue. The stifling heat of the day had subsided, making it the perfect time for a leisurely stroll. Frank took her hand as they headed along the gravel track bordered by weeping paperbarks and livistona palms.

"I guess this means our honeymoon is officially over," she said.

He slipped his arm around her shoulders and kissed the top of her head. "I guess so. But I'll never forget it, my love."

She put her arm around his waist. "Neither will I. It was the best two weeks of my life."

"It *was* special. Maybe we can go back every year on our anniversary."

She smiled. "That's a wonderful idea. I'd love to do that."

"Well, we'll see what we can do about it."

"I guess it depends on how everything is doing here," she said, trying to match her stride to his, although he was already walking slowly.

"Yes, it does." He let out a heavy sigh. "I'm not convinced the cattle drives and eco tents are going to be enough to get us through. Julian found a buyer for that last shipment of cattle, but it only just covered costs. I'm praying the government will lift the ban on live exports sometime soon, but I don't see that happening for a while."

Maggie frowned. "But you weren't granted the stay for the licensing requirements."

"No, but the silver living with the ban is that it's given us time to get things in order. We should be ready to go whenever the ban's lifted."

"Without the need to bribe that officer."

"Yes. Without the need for any bribes. Not that I would have considered it."

"I know you wouldn't, my love. Have you thought any further about reporting him? What was his name? Shepherd?"

"Yes, that's him." Frank drew a slow breath. "I truly doubt it would go anywhere. If we reported him, there's no proof he tried to bribe me."

"But he might have tried it with others."

"I guess that's possible. I'll ask around if I get the chance."

They continued in silence for a few moments. A flock of white cockatoos flew across in front of them and settled onto a branch of a paperbark tree. Somewhere, a kookaburra laughed.

It might not be Broome with its endless, white, sandy beach, but this was home, and she loved it.

They turned a corner and the homestead, a large, old home shaded by eucalyptus and bauhinias, came into view.

Frank rubbed her arm. "Here we are, my love. Are you ready?"

She inhaled slowly and smiled. "Yes."

~

Frank knew the family had planned more than a simple welcome home dinner. Julian had told him they were throwing Maggie a surprise birthday party and he couldn't have been more pleased. He sensed Maggie was a little anxious about how she'd be received by the family, although she hadn't said so. She didn't have to. He could read her like a book.

He hoped the surprise party would set her at ease, because as far as he knew, the whole family was delighted she was now part of the Goddard clan. She was now Maggie Goddard. He liked the sound of that. As he smiled, his heart warmed. She was the best thing that had happened to him in a long time, and perhaps ever.

As they approached the homestead, there was no hint of a party. In fact, it seemed unusually quiet, but when they reached the bottom of the stairs, Issie, his three-year-old granddaughter, appeared at the top, her blue eyes lighting up. She raced down the steps, her wavy blonde hair bouncing on her shoulders, and launched herself at him. "Grandpa! You're home!"

He laughed as he picked her up and hugged her. "Yes, Issie, we're home. It's good to see you. Have you been a good girl for mummy while we've been away?"

"Yes. And I've been helping with—" She slapped her hand over her mouth, stifling a giggle as she looked at Maggie, her eyes wide.

He laughed again and hugged her tightly. "It's okay, sweetie. You can tell me later what you've been doing. Now, are you going to give Maggie a hug, too?" He set her down on the ground.

Issie peered up at Maggie. "What am I going to call you?"

Maggie smiled. "My grandson calls me Nan. How does that sound?"

"Sounds fine to me," she replied, reaching up for a hug.

As Maggie met Frank's gaze briefly before bending down to hug his granddaughter, he winked, and when Issie took both their hands and the trio walked up the stairs together, his heart warmed. He smiled over Issie's head to Maggie as a deep sense of peace washed over him.

But the peace was momentary. When they reached the back of the house, it was unusually quiet until the rest of his family jumped out from behind the furniture amidst shouts of "Happy Birthday, Maggie!" while blowing hooters and releasing party poppers that filled the room with colourful streamers and lots of laughter.

Maggie faced him, her eyes bright. "Did you know about this?"

He shrugged as a grin spread across his face "Maybe."

She chuckled and then began greeting his family in turn while he stood back and watched. Of course, the menfolk were more reserved than the women. While she hugged Janella, Olivia and Sasha, his eleven-year-old granddaughter, who each returned her hug with a big one of their own, the men simply gave her a quick hug and a peck on the cheek and then stood back. Caleb, who was now almost as tall as his father, Julian, although much leaner, looked uncomfortable and awkward when she tried to hug him, but when she stepped back and smiled and said something Frank couldn't quite hear, Caleb seemed to relax. Considering what he'd been through, the boy was doing well, and Frank was looking forward to picking up their daily Bible reading sessions.

But someone was missing. *Where was Serena?*

CHAPTER 4

Facing the wall and curled in the foetal position, Serena lay on her bed with her eyes squeezed shut in an attempt to stem the flow of tears she hadn't been able to quell for some time. She should be out there celebrating her mother's birthday, but she couldn't face it. They'd all been so good to her over the past two weeks, Janella and Olivia in particular, but she felt flat. Lost. Empty.

Several times she'd considered ending it all. What purpose was there in living? Her life as she knew it was over. There'd be no more jaunts around the world as a foreign correspondent. Who would want to see her disfigured face on their television? Danny, her station manager, had suggested she could write articles for their newspaper or take over the breakfast radio time slot when she was ready. He'd assured her that the public would welcome her in whatever role she felt comfortable.

But her energy was gone and she had no interest in doing either. She wanted her old life back. It wasn't fair. If she'd suffered only a broken limb and some internal injuries, she would have been fine. She would have healed and life would have returned to normal. But her cheek. *Her cheek.* She reached a hand up and felt it. Instead of smooth, healthy skin, it was rough, lumpy and horrid. Tears welled in her eyes and spilled over. She hated it. *God, why did You let this happen to me? I hate You! I hate You!* Her sobs grew into guttural weeping that came from a place deep inside.

∽

"Do you know where Serena is?" Maggie asked Janella quietly after the initial excitement had subsided and everyone began nibbling the delicious canapes laid out on the tables.

Janella's expression sobered. "In her room. She's not in a great way, Maggie."

A small breath blew from Maggie's mouth and her stomach knotted. "I guessed that when she wasn't here."

"Liv and I have done our best with her, but she seems to have slipped into a deep depression."

"I so hoped she'd turned a corner before we left. She must have been putting on a brave face so I wouldn't worry about her."

Janella nodded, her warm, brown eyes filling with empathy. "I think you're right. Almost as soon as you left, she took to her room and she's hardly been out."

Maggie grimaced. "Oh dear. And David?"

"As far as I know, she hasn't heard from him."

Maggie drew a breath. "I'll call Jeremy a little later and see if he knows anything."

"I'm so sorry, Maggie. We really wanted your homecoming to be a happy one."

Rubbing Janella's arm, Maggie gave an appreciative smile. "It is, Janella. I really appreciate you throwing this party for me. It's wonderful. It's just going to be a long journey for Serena, that's all. Thank you for looking after her."

"You're more than welcome. I only wish we could have done more."

"It's fine. There's probably not a lot anyone can do until she decides to do something for herself."

"You're probably right. It's just so sad seeing her this way."

"I know." Maggie let out a heavy sigh. "I'll go and see her soon."

"She's in the guest room down the hallway. Dinner's in about twenty minutes but have something to nibble and drink first."

"Thanks. It's a lovely spread, Janella. You're such a good cook."

Janella smiled proudly. "Thank you. Sasha helped, of course."

"I'll have to thank her as well."

Janella's smile widened. "She'd appreciate that."

Frank approached and slipped a glass of fruit punch into Maggie's hand. "Have this, my love. All you've been doing is talking. You must be dry."

Accepting it gratefully, she smiled and took a sip. "Thanks, this is just what I needed."

He slipped an arm around her shoulders and kissed her lightly on the top of her head. "You're welcome, my love."

"Looks like you two had a good time away," Janella said, her amused gaze shifting between them.

He grinned. "The best."

Maggie leaned into him as memories of their honeymoon flashed through her mind, filling her with warmth. For a moment she forgot about Serena, but then those memories faded and were replaced by images of her daughter lying on her bed and the moment passed. Tilting her face towards his, she said softly, "Serena's not doing too well."

His expression stilled and grew serious. "She'll do better now that you're here, my love."

Maggie shrugged. "That's really kind, but I'm not so sure."

"I am," he said with confidence.

She loved his confidence but didn't share it. Only a touch from God would change Serena's heart and how she saw herself. Maggie could only pray that He would gently woo her back to Himself, that the eyes of her heart would open to His amazing love and grace, and that she wouldn't blame Him for what had happened to her.

As a young girl, Serena had given her heart to God and had been an ardent believer, but her faith had never been fully tested until she went to university and was faced with differing world views and belief systems. Maggie wasn't sure what her daughter believed anymore, but that didn't matter. The only way she would ever experience true peace was by returning to the God of peace, and that would require a shifting of her heart, a shifting that only the Holy Spirit could initiate. But in the meantime, she'd do what she could, but she sensed she was going to need a good measure of grace and God-given patience.

She took another sip of her drink. "I'll finish this and then go see her."

"Okay, my love. But don't miss dinner. It smells scrumptious."

"It sure does." Maggie turned to Janella. "Can I smell a pig roasting?"

Janella nodded. "Yes. The boys have been looking after the spit out the back. We're going to eat out there if the storm doesn't hit. We might be lucky," she said, glancing outside.

"Hopefully," Maggie said. "Anyway, if you'll excuse me…"

"Sure. Go ahead. It would be nice if you could get her to join us."

"I'll do my best." Maggie smiled and then squeezed Frank's hand. "I'll be back shortly."

He bent down and kissed her lightly on the forehead. "I'll be praying for you."

"Thank you." She gave another smile and handed him her empty glass before leaving him and walking down the hallway. As the noise faded behind her, she swallowed hard, and reaching the guest room, she paused to pray. *Lord, please give me the right words to say to Serena. My heart aches for her, but I know that until she makes peace with You, she won't know true peace. Lord, please grant me wisdom. In Jesus' precious name. Amen.*

Inhaling deeply, she knocked softly on the door. "Serena, it's Mum. Can I come in?"

Silence.

She knocked again, a little louder. "Serena?"

No answer. Maggie quietly turned the handle and opened the door just enough to peer inside. Serena was curled on the bed with her face to the wall. Pain squeezed Maggie's heart.

She pushed the door open further and walked quietly to the bed, and perching on the edge, placed her hand gently on Serena's back. "Hey sweetheart. I'm here. How are you doing?"

Serena shifted her shoulders slightly as if she was shrugging but didn't turn around. "No good." Her voice was raspy. Maggie guessed she'd been crying.

"You'll get through this, sweetheart. Let me give you a hug."

She waited a moment, and just when she thought Serena wasn't going to move, she sat up and threw her arms around Maggie's neck and burst into tears. Not wanting to hurt her, Maggie held her gently and let her sob against her chest while she fought her own tears.

Minutes passed. Sounds of laughter drifted in from the back of the house along with the aroma of roasting pig. Eventually, Serena's sobs subsided and Maggie handed her a tissue, which she took.

She dabbed her eyes. "I'm sorry, Mum. I can't seem to get out of this black hole I'm in."

"I think that's understandable, sweetie. You can't see past this, but you will, in time. I'm here for you. I'll do whatever I can to help."

Serena sniffed. "Thank you, but I don't know what you can do. You can't give me my face back." Her words dropped like stones into the suddenly silent room.

Maggie inhaled slowly, her heart filled with anguish. "No, I can't do that. You're right. But what's inside you is more important than what you look like."

Serena narrowed her eyes. "It's easy for you to say that."

Maggie grimaced. "I know, but I mean it." They'd been through this countless times and it took a measure of patience for her to bite her tongue. She didn't want to give Serena a sermon, so she simply hugged her and said, "I love you, Serena, regardless of how you look. And so does God. Jesus had nail-scarred hands and knows what you're going through. Come on, now, let's get you freshened up so you can join us for dinner."

"I'd rather not," Serena said, her gaze firm and steady.

"I can't make you come, Serena, but how long has it been since you were outside?"

Serena folded her arms. "Days."

"Fresh air will do you good."

Serena shrugged. "I'm happy here."

Maggie held her daughter's gaze. "Are you?"

Her shoulders drooped and fresh tears pooled in her eyes. "No."

"I thought as much." Maggie squeezed her shoulder. "Come on, get dressed and come outside. You don't need to talk to anyone unless you want to."

Seconds ticked by and Maggie prayed silently. Finally, Serena reluctantly agreed. "But I'm only doing it for you."

"That's fine. At least you're doing it. What would you like to wear?" Maggie stood and headed to the wardrobe.

"My clothes are in my suitcase."

"Right. Of course." Serena had only come for the wedding, not an extended stay. Maggie changed direction and found the suitcase on the floor and opened it. From the way the clothes were folded neatly, she gathered Serena might have been in her pyjamas the whole time since the wedding. "How long since you've showered?"

Serena shrugged offhandedly.

"Perhaps you should have one. You'll feel better," Maggie said softly.

"If you say so." The resigned, dull tone in Serena's voice tugged at Maggie's heart, but she forced herself to smile. "Good girl. Now, let me help you up."

"I don't need help."

"Okay. I'm sorry." Maggie stepped back and let Serena stand on her own, recalling that she'd told her David had treated her like a helpless child and she didn't like it. Maggie needed to remember that, but it was hard when Serena was acting like one.

"I can shower and dress on my own," she said, snatching the gown from the back of the door.

"All right. If you need any help, call. I'll be out the back, but I'll keep an ear open."

"Whatever. I won't be staying long."

Maggie frowned. "Do you mean at dinner, or here?"

"Both."

Maggie's heart plummeted. Serena had always known how to pull her strings—the terrorist blast hadn't stolen that from her. "Let's talk about it later, sweetheart, and sort out what to do. Are you sure you don't need help?" Maggie asked as Serena headed to the door.

Turning slowly, Serena glared at her.

Maggie groaned and stepped closer, rubbing her arm. "Sorry. I forgot."

Serena blew out a long breath and met her gaze. "I'm sorry I was short."

Tears sprang to Maggie's eyes. "Come here, sweetheart." She held her arms out and Serena stepped into them. "It'll be all right. Things will get better." Kissing the side of Serena's head, Maggie thought her heart would break. Although she was an adult, Serena was still her little girl and Maggie's mother's heart wanted to make everything right for her. If she could, she would gladly swap places.

"I hope so," Serena whispered.

CHAPTER 5

Maggie kept an eye on the back door, watching for Serena. Twenty minutes had passed since she'd left her to shower and dress, and she was beginning to think she'd changed her mind. She was about to check on her when the door opened and Serena appeared, wearing a caftan type dress with aboriginal markings on it. Not her usual style of clothing, but probably quite comfortable. Her hair had been singed in the fire and was now cut short all over. It had started to grow back, but there were a few bald patches Maggie guessed might always be bare. Serena normally wore a scarf to cover the scars on her cheek, but tonight the scars were totally visible. Her cheek was discoloured and raw.

Maggie could appreciate how difficult it was for Serena to show her face to the world. She stepped towards her and gave her a hug. "You look lovely, sweetheart."

"You don't have to lie, Mum."

"I'm not. I love the caftan. The colours are lovely."

"Not to mention that they deflect attention from my face?"

Maggie smiled. "Maybe. But you're among friends, Serena. No one is going to be bothered. Honestly."

Serena released a big sigh and glanced around. "I know. But I can't help feeling self-conscious."

"I can understand that, but if people can't see past your scars, that's their problem."

Serena swung her gaze back to Maggie. "I'm not sure I can get used to people staring."

"Nobody's going to stare at you here, so let me get you a drink and something to nibble, although dinner's about to be served." Maggie steered her towards Frank who was seated with Olivia underneath the shade of a eucalypt. She picked up a drink from a table and handed it to Serena. "Here you go. It's the best punch I've tasted in a long time."

Serena lifted a brow. "I'd prefer something stronger."

Maggie chuckled. "I'm sure you would, but this is what's on offer." Reaching Frank and Olivia, she slipped her arm around Serena's waist. "Look who's here."

Frank stood and greeted Serena with a warm smile and a careful hug. "Good to see you, Serena."

Maggie was pleased when Serena replied in kind. It seemed the manners she'd been taught hadn't been lost in the blast.

Olivia also gave her a hug and said it was good to see her up and about. "I like the caftan," she said. "Where did you get it?"

Serena glanced down and shrugged. "At the markets ages ago. I've not worn it before."

"Well, it's lovely, and it must be cool."

"It feels nice on. Floaty." She reached down and felt the fabric. "It's different from the clothes I normally wear."

"Yes, I've seen you on the TV. You always look so smart."

Serena's eyes flickered. "Those days are gone."

"I'm so sorry," Olivia said, reaching her hand out. "I didn't mean—"

"It's okay. I'm just feeling sorry for myself."

"You're amongst friends here. I hope you know that."

Serena nodded as tears welled in her eyes and she turned away.

Maggie put her arm around her shoulders and stood with her. The sun was low on the horizon and the sky was now a glorious orange. The colours were so vibrant. Deep and rich, evoking emotion, pointing her to God, the Creator. She prayed silently that Serena might find Him here in this remote, rugged, beautiful land, amongst this family who had known both hardship and joy but had never doubted God's faithfulness.

Behind them, Julian cleared his throat and called everyone to attention.

Maggie turned and Serena did the same.

He was standing beside the main table filled with platters overflowing with roasted pork and vegetables. For the first time, Maggie noticed how much alike he and Frank looked. Julian's hair was thicker, while Frank's was receding and thinning, but their profiles were the same. As was their stance. Casual. Relaxed. Hands in pockets. She hadn't seen Julian quite like this before. Janella was right. God had certainly been working in his life because he no longer seemed to be the angry man who'd challenged her on her first visit to the station.

His gaze travelled around the group and then settled on her

and Frank. "Before we eat, I'd like to officially welcome back Dad and Maggie, and also wish Maggie a happy birthday for yesterday." He raised his drink and said "cheers". Everybody followed suit. "We hope you'll settle in quickly and that you'll be happy here."

Maggie smiled and gave a grateful nod.

"Let's give thanks before we eat," he said to the group. When he bowed his head, Maggie shifted closer to Frank, slipped her hand into his, and squeezed it. In the past it had been his role as head of the household to give thanks. She sensed he might be struggling, although it wasn't the first time Julian had said grace. Nevertheless, she wanted to reassure him.

When he squeezed her hand back, she sensed he was okay and she relaxed.

When Julian finished, he announced that she and Frank should go first since they were the guests of honour. Frank placed his hand on the small of her back as they approached the table. Maggie turned to check on Serena and smiled. She was talking with Olivia and seemed happy enough. It was a start, although Maggie knew it could be a façade Serena was putting on, much like she'd done at the wedding.

After filling their plates, Maggie and Frank sat at a long table covered with white tablecloths. As evening slowly descended, the lights strung between the branches came on, making it look like fairy land. With Serena on one side and Frank on the other, Maggie gazed around at her new family as they chatted and laughed together, and she thanked God once again for the many blessings He'd bestowed on her.

After the main course, she was surprised when Janella

brought out a huge birthday cake, complete with candles that somehow remained lit while she walked from the house to the table. She set the cake in front of Maggie while everybody sang 'happy birthday'. Leaning against Frank, she blinked back tears of happiness before blowing out the candles, then realised a speech was expected.

Drawing a slow breath, she stood and smiled at the expectant faces of the family. Unprepared, she took a moment to gather her thoughts before clearing her throat. "Thank you, everyone, for making this evening so special. I had no idea you were planning this, and I feel humbled by it. For a long time, the prospect of turning sixty had been daunting, but now I've realised it's just a number and that nothing has really changed. I'm still me, and although I might have a few more grey hairs than I had ten years ago, I'm grateful for good health, a wonderful husband, and a family who's welcomed me with open arms. So, thank you, everyone, especially Janella, Olivia and Sasha, for providing the amazing food, and of course, the boys for cooking it on the spit. It was wonderful. Thank you." When she raised her glass, everyone clapped before she sat down.

Frank slipped his arm around her shoulders and kissed her cheek. "You did well, my love."

"Thank you." She gave him a smile. "I guess I need to cut the cake now."

"Let me do that, Mum."

Maggie's eyes widened. Had she heard correctly? Serena was offering to cut the cake? She blinked and then smiled. "That would be great, sweetheart. Thank you."

"I need to do something." The cool tone in Serena's voice

caused an ache to tear through Maggie's heart. No doubt she was feeling bad because she hadn't done anything for her birthday. Her focus had been on herself, no one else. Not even her mother's sixtieth. It didn't matter. Offering to cut the cake was a promising step. Maggie squeezed her wrist and smiled. "I'm sure Janella has a knife."

Right on cue, Janella appeared with a large knife and a number of small plates. "Here we go."

Serena took the knife and proceeded to cut the cake, a chocolate gateau, complete with fresh cream and strawberries. Janella helped her to place the pieces on the plates and then handed them around, offering the first pieces to Frank and Maggie.

The cake was rich but scrumptious. Maggie struggled to finish her piece but battled on since it was too good to leave. "I'll put on weight if I'm not careful," she said to Frank after setting her empty plate aside.

"Not much chance of that, my love, with what I've got planned for you." His eyes twinkled.

She frowned. "Like what?"

"Oh, I can think of quite a few jobs around the place that will keep you active, like helping with the fencing. You were great at that." He winked.

"I was not. My hands ached after only a few minutes."

"But you didn't give up."

"No. I didn't. I guess I could give it another try."

Chuckling, he gave her a hug. "I was joking. But seriously, I'll love you regardless of what you do or how you look."

Their gazes held, and for a moment she forgot they were not alone. "I love you, Frank," she said softly.

He lifted his palm to her cheek and smiled into her eyes. "I love you, too."

The moment was interrupted when Issie tapped Maggie's arm and asked if she could sit on her lap. Maggie smiled. "Sure, sweetheart." Issie climbed up and leaned against her chest.

"Have you had a nice party?" Maggie asked, cuddling the little girl.

Issie nodded. "But I think I want to go to sleep soon."

Maggie chuckled as she met Frank's gaze. It seemed Issie was settling in for the evening. She was right. Within moments, her eyes had shut and her breathing had slowed. Maggie didn't mind. It was a precious moment that made her feel special. It was such a blessing to have gained four additional grandchildren.

Her gaze shifted to Serena who was now talking with Joshua and Sean, Frank's youngest son and a nephew of a similar age. She wasn't sure how that had happened, but the trio were seated on chairs around a fire and seemed settled in for the evening. Considering how Serena had sustained her injuries, Maggie wondered how she was coping with the fire. She also wondered what the future held for her. Would she reconcile with David? It would be a pity if they didn't—he was such a nice man. She doubted Serena would ever have children. She'd always been adamant that she was a career woman and had no interest in a family. But now that her career may have ended, maybe that resolve would change, too. Time would tell.

CHAPTER 6

With Serena posted overseas for much of the year, David was used to spending time on his own. Whenever she returned, they picked up where they'd left off, but this time it was different. She'd returned injured, and he'd smothered her. He knew he had, but he hadn't been able to stop himself. It was like a switch had been flicked inside him and he'd gone into carer mode.

He pushed harder up the hill. Cycling had become his escape since he'd left Serena the night before Maggie and Frank's wedding, when he'd driven all the way back to Darwin, stopping only long enough to refuel. Leaving had been a knee-jerk reaction after she turned down his proposal, a proposal that shouldn't have happened. *What had he been thinking?* She wasn't ready. He knew that, and now she wouldn't even talk to him.

His breaths came faster and sweat poured off him as he

crested the hill. Reaching East Point, he slowed and stopped. He usually kept going, but today he'd sit a while.

He got off his bike, and grabbing his drink bottle, drank greedily. The air was heavy and humid, the light breeze barely providing any relief. Seated on the bench overlooking Fanny Bay, he pulled out his phone and checked for messages. Two missed calls from Jeremy. The guy didn't give up. He'd be calling to check on him, but David didn't want to speak to him. He didn't want anything more to do with Serena or her family.

But that wasn't true. If there'd been a call or a message from her, he would have called her back immediately. *Who was he kidding?* He still loved her.

Slamming his empty drink bottle onto the ground, he folded his arms and stared across the bay as a heavy invisible weight crushed him. *Why had he been so stupid?*

A few seconds later, another rider stopped nearby. Not wanting to talk to anybody, David kept his head low as he stood and scooped up his bottle and headed to his bike, but a familiar voice calling out stopped him in his tracks. "Thought it was you. You're a hard man to get hold of, David."

His shoulders drooped. It was Jeremy, of all people.

"How are you doing, mate?" Coming closer, Serena's older brother removed his helmet.

"Good," David lied.

"I don't believe you. Word around town is that you've become a loner."

"Better than turning to the bottle." David gave a pointed look.

"You've got that one right." Jeremy groaned. "You've heard about Cliff."

"Sure have. He's made a mess of things all right. He'll do jail time if the girl dies." Cliff, Serena and Jeremy's father, had been involved in a hit and run, and the victim, a girl of only ten, was fighting for her life. He was on bail and due to face court the following week, but the situation would change drastically if the girl didn't survive.

"So, how are you really doing?" Jeremy sipped water from his drink bottle as the sun glistened on his damp, dark hair.

David returned to the seat and flopped on it. Leaning forward on his crossed elbows, he stared across the bay. "Honestly, not great."

"She does love you, you know."

Straightening, he crossed his arms and faced Jeremy. "She's got a great way of showing it. You should have heard what she said." Their last conversation reverberated in his brain like an echo that played over and over.

Jeremy rolled his eyes. "I can imagine. That sister of mine has an acid tongue at times. I know—I've borne the brunt of it, but she doesn't mean it."

"I'm not so sure about that. She was pretty adamant when she told me to pack my bags."

"Well, according to Mum, she's not doing too well, either. I wouldn't give up on her yet."

David released a heavy breath. "I've put in for a transfer."

"Really? Where to?" Jeremy sat beside him.

"Anywhere. I need to get away."

"Maybe time away would do you good, although some might see it as running."

David's eyes narrowed. "I'm not running."

"Are you sure about that?"

Seconds passed. "Yes."

"Stay, then."

David shrugged. "I can't live in the same town as Serena if we're not together."

"It'll be harder to get her back if you're not here."

David knew the truth of that. Maybe he should stay and fight for her. But after months of caring for her following the blast, when he'd willingly given everything up for her, only to have her throw it all back at him… He was tired. He'd pushed her too hard and now he'd lost her. "I don't know, mate. I think I need to go, at least for a while."

Jeremy remained silent for a moment, and then said, "Why don't you come around for dinner tonight? It's curry night, and I know how much you like a good, hot curry."

David thought about it for a moment but then replied, "It's tempting, but I'm on call tonight. Sorry."

Jeremy's brow lifted. "Are you back at work?"

"Yeah. There's no reason for me not to be working now." He was a firefighter and had taken indefinite leave to look after Serena.

"You can still come if you're on call."

David groaned at the guy's persistence. "I'll think about it."

"Good, but I'm guessing you're saying that to shut me up. You'd really be welcome, mate, so don't be a stranger. Just because my sister jerked you around doesn't mean we can't be friends."

"All right. I'll think about it."

Jeremy clapped him on the back. "Good man. See you about six."

"Maybe."

"That's as good as a yes. I'd best get back. The heat's not letting up, is it?"

"No. At least the cyclone fizzled out."

"Yes, that was a blessing."

David frowned. "Are you religious?"

"No, but I believe in God. Don't you?"

David shrugged and blew out a long, deep breath. "I'm not sure anymore."

"Let's have a conversation about that some time." Jeremy clipped up his helmet and climbed onto his bike. "See you tonight."

David gave a non-committal wave as he rode off. He doubted he'd go, although Emma's curries were the best and he hadn't been eating well over the past couple of weeks. Two-minute noodles, frozen meals, baked beans. Home-made curry actually sounded good. But did he want to spend time with Serena's brother, especially if he was going to talk about God? He shrugged. It could be interesting. Maybe he would.

After a slow ride back to the apartment he'd shared with Serena for the last six years, he jumped into the shower. When his phone rang while he was towelling his hair, he almost ignored it, but a glance told him it was work. He picked it up and answered.

"Hey, Dave." It was his boss, Reggie. "How do you feel about going south? The New South Wales Fire Service has called for help and I thought you might be keen to go."

David brightened. Without hesitating, he answered, "Yeah, mate. Count me in." He'd been watching the fire situation down south for a while and wondered if a call for help would come. This could be the answer to his time out. "Who else is going?"

"Troy and Robbo so far. I'm still contacting everyone."

"When do they want us?"

"Immediately."

"So, today?"

"Yes. The flight leaves at three p.m."

David checked the time. It was only twelve. Plenty of time to pack. "I'll be there."

"Good man. See you then."

That settled that. No curry tonight. He quickly sent Jeremy a text and began packing. Not that he'd need much. There'd be no down time with a fire front as large as this one. He could already feel the adrenaline building.

CHAPTER 7

Maggie set her coffee mug on the table and gazed across the lagoon. The sun had recently set and the sky was still awash with brilliant oranges, pinks and crimsons. She'd come to love this time of evening. It was a time to share the simple pleasures with Frank after he returned from working all day out in the paddocks or the sheds, because even though he'd promised to slow down, he'd gotten straight back into it the day after they returned from their honeymoon.

At first, she hadn't been sure what to do with her time. Having taken indefinite leave from her job, and with nothing more specific to be doing other than writing Clara Goddard's biography and spending time with Serena, she'd taken to spending her days engrossed in a good book, but a sense of guilt overtook her whenever she opened one. It almost seemed wrong when she knew how hard Janella and Olivia worked, but she wouldn't intrude, although she was considering offering her help with the eco tents if everyone was agreeable. She also wanted to offer money to develop the basic set-up into something grander but was anxious about discussing it with Frank.

Like Julian, she believed that Goddard Downs should embrace tourism with open arms. Other stations had successfully incorporated it into their business structure, and she didn't see any good reason why Goddard Downs shouldn't. The only obstacle was Frank. While he was happy dipping his toe in with the overnight cattle drives and eco tents, he'd refused to discuss anything beyond that. She'd need to choose the right moment to raise the subject with him. The last thing she wanted was to cause any friction between them.

But tonight wasn't the time—something else was on her mind. They'd had their first disagreement that morning. Frank had assumed they'd take all their meals at the homestead. While she was happy to eat there occasionally, she'd assumed they'd mostly have their meals alone at the cabin. It was their home, after all, and they were newlyweds.

They'd both said words they immediately regretted, and after apologising, they reached a compromise, agreeing to have breakfast and lunch at the cabin and to share dinner twice a week with the family at the homestead. "We can always invite them here sometimes," she'd said.

"I hadn't thought about that, but I guess we could," he'd conceded.

They'd just enjoyed their first dinner on their own, and now, with the sky ablaze with colour and the sounds of evening filling the air, she reached out and took his hand across the table. "I enjoyed our meal together, Frank. I'm sorry about this morning."

He massaged the top of her hand with his thumb as he turned his head, sending a shiver down her spine as their gazes connected. "So am I, my love. I shouldn't have gotten so heated."

She smiled. "Are you really happy to eat here together and not be with the family?"

"It's an adjustment for sure, but not one I can't make. I hadn't thought about it, that's all."

"I know not being with the family is a big change for you, so thank you."

"There's no need to thank me. You're my wife, and I love sitting out here with you. But now, what else is on that mind of yours? I can see the cogs ticking." He drew circles on her hand with his finger, his eyes twinkling.

Maggie chuckled. For a man, he was quite intuitive. It didn't help that she wore her heart on her sleeve. "You're right. I do have a few things on my mind."

"Do we need another coffee?"

She chuckled again. "No." But she smiled at his thoughtfulness.

"Okay, what have you got?"

She drew a deep breath. What to raise first? Jeremy's phone call, church, or getting to know the neighbours? She decided to go with the easy one first. Church. "Is there any way we can start going to church? I know the closest one is in Kununurra, and right now we'd have to take the helicopter, but I'd like to go, if not every week, perhaps every second one."

"I don't see why not. We could have lunch with Sarah, Mick and Mum, and do some sightseeing on the way back."

"That would be lovely. Thank you. I've missed worship these past couple of months."

"We should have made the effort to go before now. I guess I've gotten used to not going, but I agree that having regular fellowship is important. The rest of the family might even decide to go."

"It might be good for them. I sometimes wonder if they shouldn't have more contact with others. Especially the kids."

Frank's brows twitched.

She gulped. Had she overstepped the mark? What right did she have to make comments like that? Four generations had lived here at Goddard Downs and survived. More than survived. Thrived. Their family was close knit. Did they really need contact with outsiders? "I'm sorry, Frank. I shouldn't have said that. It's not my place."

"No, you're right. It would probably do them good. Caleb's supposed to be going to boarding school next year but he doesn't want to go. We all think he should. He's barely had any direct contact with boys his age."

"He seems to be doing well, though."

Frank nodded. "Yes. I'm proud of the way he's coming along."

"That's partly because of you, Frank. I see the way you two get on and it warms my heart so. He's very fortunate to have you as his grandpa."

"You're too kind, Maggie, but thank you."

They shared a moment of silence before she broached the next topic, one she hoped wouldn't open a bag of worms. "Do you ever mix with your neighbours? I know they aren't close by, but do you ever get together with them?"

When Frank drew a slow breath, she wondered if she had overstepped. He stretched his legs and stared at the lagoon. "Once again, we used to. When Esther was alive. She used to organise a gathering every few months."

Maggie gulped. The bag was well and truly open. "I'm sorry, Frank. I seem to be putting my foot in my mouth every time I speak."

He swung his gaze to her. "No, Maggie. It's fine. We should be able to talk about all these things, and I want you to feel that this is your home. This place is full of memories, that's for sure, and they all hold a special place, but you and I are building our own memories. We need to carve our own path."

"I'm so glad to hear you say that. So…do you think we could organise a get together sometime soon? I'd really like to meet our neighbours."

He nodded. "I think it's a wonderful idea. It's been way too long since we've seen each other. We've been so focused on survival that we've overlooked being neighbourly. I'll speak to Janella and Liv about it tomorrow."

She bit back her immediate response. Of course Janella and Olivia should be the ones to organise it. She didn't know the neighbours, but despite that, she'd hoped it could have been her project. She finally said, "Since I mentioned it, I'm happy to help."

He patted her hand. "And I'm sure they'll welcome it. Now, what's next?"

She threw her head back and laughed. "How did you know there was something else?"

"Oh, I have a way."

"I know you do." She gazed into his blue eyes as she wove her hand into his. It still amazed her that she'd fallen so deeply in love with this man, and he with her. He made her insides turn to flame whenever she stared into his eyes. She almost forgot what she was about to say, but then remembered. Clearing her throat, the words tumbled out. "Jeremy telephoned today. He bumped into David this morning, but only a short time later, David got called away to help with the fires down south. Jeremy thought Serena should know he's gone. He also mentioned that David didn't seem to be in a good frame of mind, and he got the feeling he could implode. Not as bad as Cliff, but definitely hurting." She paused and took a breath. "It's probably not a good state of mind to be in when fighting fires."

"You're worried about him?"

She nodded. "He could easily put himself in harm's way—take risks he shouldn't. All because Serena rejected him. I need to talk with her about him, but each time I try, she changes the subject."

Frank rubbed her hand. "She'll come around, you'll see."

"I certainly hope so. She's talking about going back to Darwin, but she can't go on her own." Maggie paused before continuing. "I'd have to go with her, but I don't want to leave you."

"I'd go with you, Maggie."

"But what about the station?"

"The boys would manage without me."

Relief filled her. "That would be great. I don't want us to be separated, Frank, but I can't leave Serena, either."

"I understand, my love. But you never know, she might decide to stay. Let me chat with her."

Maggie smiled. Sharing the responsibility with Frank was such a relief. He was so different from Cliff, who'd barely given her any support with the children. "That would be great. She seems to respect you."

He chuckled and rubbed the back of his neck. "I don't know about that, but at least she's polite with me. She also seems to be getting on with Josh and Sean, so perhaps she might like to help with the cattle drives."

Maggie laughed. "As far as I know, she's never ridden a horse."

He chuckled again. "Well, maybe it's time she learned how. So, what's the other thing?"

Maggie frowned. How did he know she had something else on her mind? She hadn't planned on raising the tourism issue tonight. "What makes you think there's something else?"

"Oh, I can just tell something's bothering you. Don't ask how."

"Hmmm." She shifted in her chair. "Okay. Well yes, there is something. I'd like to help with the eco tents."

His head angled. "I don't see why there'd be a problem with that."

"That's not all." Maggie swallowed hard. "You know I have money…"

Frank's brows knitted. "Yes…"

"I…I'm not sure I should be saying this."

"Just say it, Maggie."

"Okay. You know how I visited a number of other stations when I was doing my research?"

He nodded. "I think I know where this is going."

"Hear me out."

"I'm listening." He tapped a finger on the table, his gaze narrowing.

She tried to ignore it and continued. "A fair number have embraced tourism, like Brampton Downs. That was an amazing place, don't you agree?"

"For a wedding, yes."

"I think we could do something like that here. Not so grand, but there's a demand for top quality guest lodgings in the Kimberley. I think it would complement the cattle drives and the eco tents, giving people more options. And they'd love it here." She paused. "How am I doing?"

He lifted a brow. "If you were pitching to anyone but me, I'd say you were doing great. But you're not going to win me over, Maggie. I don't want Goddard Downs to lose its character. We're a family run cattle station, not some fancy tourist destination."

She tried to disguise her disappointment. "I thought you'd say that. That's why I wasn't going to mention it tonight."

"I'm sorry I pushed."

She released a breath. She wasn't going to get anywhere with him, which was such a pity because it could be great.

He took both her hands in his and looked deep into her eyes. "I appreciate your offer, Maggie, but I don't think it's what the Lord wants for us."

"Are you sure about that? Are you sure you're not set in your ways and simply don't like change?" She kept her voice light and made it sound as if she was teasing him, but part of her did actually think it was true.

"Well, there's a red flag to a bull if I might say so." His eyes twinkled.

"Sorry. I couldn't help it." She chuckled, thankful he hadn't taken her comment seriously. "If you change your mind, the offer's there."

"Thank you. Maybe we can think of a better use for your money."

"Like what?"

"I'm not sure. Let's pray about it."

"That's a wonderful idea. And let's pray about all the things we've talked about. There are so many possibilities and things to look forward to."

"Yes, but as long as we're together, my love, that's all I need." His hand came up to caress her cheek.

"Oh Frank, you turn me to mush."

He chuckled. "And you, my dear, make every day brighter."

She laughed. "We're just a couple of old romantics, aren't we?"

"Who are you calling old?"

"No one."

"Good!" He squeezed her hand and smiled. "Shall we pray?"

"Yes." Maggie bowed her head, and as Frank began to pray, his voice calm and sincere, peace settled over her.

"Our dear Lord and Heavenly Father, we come before You in awe of who You are. We acknowledge that in You we live and breathe and have our being. We thank You for bringing us together and for the great love we have for each other, but right now, on our hearts are many things. You know them already, but Lord, we bring them to You and ask that You hear our prayers. Firstly, we bring Serena before You. Let her heart be open to You. May she see the depth of Your love for her and be comforted by that. Let her see that You have a plan for her, and that despite her injuries, her life can have meaning and purpose. *We* know that, Lord, but we pray that she might see that, too.

"And Lord, we also pray for David. Keep him safe as he fights these terrible fires down south, but more than that, Lord, we pray that he will come to know You as well. That amidst his heartache and confusion, he will turn to You, the great Healer. Reveal Yourself to him, Lord, we pray.

"And lastly, we commit the future of Goddard Downs to You. You know how much the station means to me, and how much the live export ban is hurting us. Show us the way forward, and help me to welcome change if that's what's needed. In Your precious Son's name, we pray. Amen."

Maggie cleared her throat. "Lord, I thank You for bringing Frank into my life. I feel so blessed to have him as my husband. Show me how I can support and help him through these difficult times, and Lord, as Frank has already prayed, we ask that You draw Serena and David to Yourself. Open the eyes of their hearts that they might see Jesus and come to experience the peace that comes from a right relationship with You. In Jesus' precious name. Amen."

When Maggie opened her eyes, the sky had turned from orange to black and was now filled with twinkling stars. It was almost as if God had held out His hand and scattered them onto a blank canvas like fairy dust. Her heart filled with the assurance that not only had He heard their prayers, but that He would answer them.

CHAPTER 8

David arrived in the small town of Mulladoola on the south coast of New South Wales at midnight. He and ten others from Darwin had flown to Canberra that afternoon and were transported the remaining distance by truck. After a short briefing, they were told to grab a few hours of sleep and report for duty at four a.m.

Although it was midnight, smoke hung heavily in the air, and the horizon was tinged a deep orange. Although it was the middle of the night, the temperature still hovered in the low thirties and the forecast was for another day of extreme temperatures and high winds. The worst combination with the land tinder dry.

He bunked down on a stretcher in the makeshift camp and closed his eyes, but sleep evaded him. The next few days would demand much of him physically, but he was prepared. This was his job. What he'd trained for. *And he hoped it would help keep his mind off Serena.*

When sleep finally came, it was fitful and filled with images of her and the blast that almost killed her in Paris. He hadn't been there when it happened, but the images were so vivid, he could have been. He pictured the scene completely and it filled him with immense sadness. Other images besieged his subconscious as well. Another blast. Another fire. So real, yet so far away. The images, locked in his sub-conscious, only came to him in his dreams, but when he was awake, he knew he'd dreamed of the fire that killed his mother and siblings, although he couldn't remember it. He'd only been four at the time, and somehow, he and his father had survived.

The lights came on at four, turning night into day with the flick of a switch, and ten minutes later, he was dressed and ready to go. The pale fingers of dawn were lighting the night sky when he lined up outside with the other men for breakfast. An eerie quiet filled the air, as if everyone was preparing themselves for what lay ahead.

With breakfast over, instructions were given. He was to join the front line along the western side of the ridge. The team's task was to stop the fire from crossing the ridge and entering the town that lay beyond it. The residents in the area had been told to leave, but some had ignored the instructions and had stayed to protect their homes. It was foolhardy. He wasn't a praying man, but he hoped the people would see sense and leave before it was too late. Anyone who thought they could outsmart a raging fire wasn't thinking straight.

∼

FRANK FOUND Serena sitting on the homestead's verandah the

following morning, staring into the distance. Although he wasn't trying to be quiet, she didn't appear to notice his approach until he stood right beside her. "Mind if I join you?" he asked softly when she looked up.

She shrugged offhandedly. "I'm not good company."

"I don't mind." He sat on a rocker and waited for her to speak.

"Did Mum send you?" Her gaze narrowed.

"No."

"Why are you here, then?"

"I thought you might like someone different to chat with."

She folded her arms. "What I need is time alone."

"Would you like me to go?"

"I didn't say that."

"Okay." He drummed his fingers on his thighs. She was pricklier than she'd been with him before. "Did you know that David's gone south to fight the fires?"

Her eyes flickered. "No. How do you know that?"

"Jeremy saw him before he left and told your mother."

"Oh."

"How do you feel about that?"

"We're not together anymore, so it doesn't affect me." Her gaze held steady, as if she were challenging him to disagree. Her eyes were a similar shape and colour to Maggie's, but where Maggie's were often filled with merriment, Serena's held pain. The news affected her greatly, although she wouldn't admit it.

"It's still okay to care, Serena," he said.

She tore her gaze away.

Moments passed. Finally, she said softly, "Okay. I do care,

but I can't marry him, now or ever. Not looking like this." She lifted a hand to her cheek.

"I'm sure he doesn't care what you look like."

"I do. But there's more to it than that. He feels guilty that he and his father were the only ones from his family to survive the fire that destroyed their home when he was four."

"Oh." Frank angled his head. "I didn't know that."

"Looking after me is his way of dealing with his guilt."

"And that's why he became a firefighter," Frank said.

"Yes."

"I'm sure it wasn't simply guilt that made him propose."

She shrugged and shifted in the chair. "I don't know."

A deep sadness gripped Frank's heart. He hadn't known what happened to David's family. Maggie mustn't have known either, or else she would have told him, but he was sure David loved Serena and that it wasn't simply guilt that drove him to propose. If only she could open herself to love, and not just the love of a man. To the love of God, who also loved her regardless of what she looked like because she was His child.

"Don't waste your life, Serena. You survived that blast when you could have died. You came out of it with scarring, but you're alive. Life is precious, even if you're carrying scars. I'm sure David would want you to see that, too. He'd probably give anything to have his family back, much like I'd—" He stopped mid-sentence, his words dangling in the air. He was about to say he'd give anything to have Esther back, but that wasn't the right thing to say now that he was married to Maggie. He quickly changed tack. "Caleb had survivor's guilt."

She frowned. "Your grandson?"

Frank nodded. "Yes. For many years he carried the blame

for his grandmother's death." He told her the story of the day Esther died in the raging floodwaters.

"I had no idea," Serena said once he'd finished. "Mum never told me. I'm so sorry."

"Grief does strange things to us and we all react differently, but it doesn't change the fact that things happen. All the time. Not many of us get through life unscathed by something or other. Sometimes it takes a while to work through it, and sometimes it's good to talk about it rather than bottling how you feel. I'm sure your psychologist told you that."

"I only went once, but yes."

"And have you talked about it?"

She shrugged. "There's not much to talk about. I'm scarred and somehow I've got to deal with it."

"Put in a nutshell, yes, but it's also a grieving process you're going through. You've suffered a loss, much like David did, and much like Caleb and I did. You might not have lost someone, but you lost your identity. Or you think you have. But don't let how you look define you. If you do, you've let those terrorists win, and I'm sure you don't want that."

"I hadn't thought about it that way. Of course I don't."

"It might take time to get comfortable with how you look, but your mother and I are both praying that one day soon you'll look in the mirror and not even see those scars. Instead, you'll see a beautiful young woman full of potential and God-given talent." He shifted closer and smiled.

"That's a nice sentiment, but I doubt that will ever happen."

"It will if you see yourself how God does. You know, the best therapy would be to read the Bible."

Serena raised a brow. "The Bible?"

"Yes. It's the story of God's amazing love. He doesn't love us because of how we look, what we do, or how clever we are. He loves us because we're His children and His love is unconditional. To have real peace, we need to embrace that truth. God loves us just the way we are, warts and all."

Serena folded her arms and gazed into the distance. "I used to believe in Him until I saw all the hatred in the world. Being a journalist, you get to see some horrible stuff. If He's real, I don't understand why He lets it happen."

"It's not His fault. We live in a fallen world, far different to what He'd planned. He gave mankind freedom to choose how to live. If He withdrew that freedom, we'd be no more than puppets. He'll bring the world as we know it to an end one of these days, but in the meantime, He gives everyone the opportunity to choose to live for Him. He won't stop all the bad things from happening, but He does give strength to those who trust Him to rise above them."

She let out a heavy sigh. "I need time on my own to work through everything. Since the day I woke up in the hospital, someone's been with me almost twenty-four seven and I feel suffocated."

"You're welcome to stay here. There's plenty of space and I'm sure everyone would respect your need to be alone."

She offered him a small smile. "Thanks. Let me think about it?"

"Sure. And here's something else to think about. The boys are planning a practice cattle drive when the weather allows. Would you be interested?"

"You mean, ride a horse? Camp out?"

He nodded.

She crossed her arms. "I don't think so."

"I thought you were the adventurous type."

"I used to be."

"I doubt any of the horses would notice your scars."

She pursed her lips, but for the first time, her eyes held a sparkle. Only a small one, but a sparkle all the same. "Funny."

"Think about it?"

She shrugged. "Maybe. I'll see."

Frank pushed to his feet. "That's all I can ask for. Don't give up, Serena. You've got your whole life ahead of you. Don't let those terrorists snatch it from you." He squeezed her shoulder before leaving, hopeful that his words might have reached her in some small way.

∽

FRANK'S PARTING words reverberated in Serena's mind. He was right. The terrorists had snatched life as she knew it from her. In an instant, when the blast ripped through that building, everything had changed. Her chin jutted defiantly. What right did they have to destroy the lives of innocent people? It was despicable. They didn't deserve to live. As far as she knew, only two suspects had been arrested and charged. *Two!* Nineteen people had died, and countless others, like her, had been injured. Where was the justice in that?

Anger seethed through her as a flock of galahs soared overhead with not a care in the world. What would it be like to live that way? She'd never know. Her face was scarred for life. The doctors had said the redness would fade, and future skin grafts might help a little, but the skin would always be rough and deeply rutted. She doubted she'd ever look in a mirror and not be repulsed. That there'd ever be a time when she'd be comfortable in her own skin again.

A Bible verse she'd learned long ago drifted into her thoughts. *The Lord does not look at the things people look at. People look at the outward appearance, but the Lord looks at the heart.* She sighed. That might be, but if He looked at her heart right now, He'd see only bitterness and anger. She couldn't continue that way, she knew that. She wouldn't let those terrorists destroy her life, but right now she had no idea how to climb out of the miry pit that held her captive.

Perhaps she should stay and go on the cattle drive. She would have jumped at the chance before the blast. Maybe that could be the first step to reclaiming her life. Not that she could ride a horse, and maybe it was silly to think she could. Her ankle wasn't fully healed and she still felt physically weak, but the idea of camping out under the stars did appeal.

She and David used to enjoy camping out. In fact, some of their best times together had been when they'd packed their camping gear into the car and headed to the Kakadu or one of the other local national parks. But she wouldn't think about those times, because they would make her think of him, and thoughts of him made her sad. Her shoulders drooped. It was too late. Frank's news hadn't surprised her. Of course David would have jumped at the chance to fight those raging fires down south. The more dangerous the fire, the better, as far as he was concerned. They'd always argued over that. But then, she had no leg to stand on. She'd never been one to avoid risk, either. She felt her face. If only she'd been less gung-ho and taken the option to stay further away from the danger zone. But it was too late now.

It's never too late, Serena...

She straightened. Where had that come from? She looked around, but no one was there.

CHAPTER 9

Later the following morning, after finishing her chores, Maggie grabbed her book and wandered over to the homestead to spend time with Serena. Frank was out on the western boundary checking the fence line with Julian and said he wouldn't be back until dinner. He'd promised to take the full weekend off and they'd fly into Kununurra late Saturday afternoon and stay with Sarah and Mick overnight, and then go to church on Sunday before coming home.

Although they'd only been back from their honeymoon less than a week, she was already looking forward to the change of scenery. Not that she was unhappy. Not at all. Married life was wonderful, but there was something about knowing she couldn't easily go into town to grab a few items from the grocery store or drop into a café for a coffee and a chat with a friend. It was something she would learn to deal with. It was part and parcel of being married to a cattle man, but the thought nibbled at the back of her mind… *would she ever get bored?*

No. She'd make sure of that, but it would certainly be easier if she was more involved in the day to day activities of the station rather than staying at the cabin all day as if she were on vacation. Frank had said he'd speak with Janella and Olivia about organising a get together with the neighbours, so she could work on that, and she'd also offer her help with the eco tents, not that there was much to do to prepare them for the tourist season. Six tents had already been erected, and as far as she knew, they only needed furnishing. Perhaps she could offer to do that. And perhaps she could ask Serena to help her. *If Serena planned on staying.*

Everything would change if Serena didn't amend her decision to return to Darwin. Although Frank had said he'd go with Maggie, she knew he'd soon get bored and want to return to Goddard Downs. It had been different when she'd returned from Paris and he'd stayed in town for weeks—he was courting her. Now that they were married, there was no reason for him to go into the city unless it was on business.

She sighed as she strolled along the track. She was worrying about all these things when she should be trusting God to work them out. Why was it so hard to do that? She had no doubt about God's love for her and her family, so why did anxiety nibble away at that trust so often? *Lord, please help me to trust You more. Don't let my heart grow anxious. Instead, fill it with Your peace as I hand all my cares to You. You, Lord, are trustworthy, and I choose to walk in Your ways. Please help me to do that each and every day.*

Rounding the last corner, the homestead came into view.

Olivia was outside tending the vegetable garden, while nearby, Isobel and William were running around with the chickens. Their infectious laughter warmed Maggie's heart and made her smile.

Olivia glanced up and waved as Maggie approached. "Hey, Maggie. How are you today?" She wiped her brow with the back of her sleeve, smearing dirt on her forehead.

"Great, thanks. Would you like a hand?"

"That would be lovely, but you'll get dirty."

"Oh, a bit of dirt never hurt anyone." Stepping through the gate, Maggie pulled up her sleeves and inspected the garden. It was much larger than the average backyard veggie patch but was filled with all the normal vegetables of beans, tomatoes and sweet corn. There was also a green house where seedlings were raised, ready to plant once the wet season ended. "What would you like me to do?"

"How do you feel about weeding? It's a never-ending job."

Maggie chuckled. "I can imagine. Weeds absolutely love this climate."

"They sure do. Grab some gloves and tools from the shed and start wherever you want. I'll have to finish up soon, I'm sorry. I've got a call coming in from a supplier I need to take."

"No problem. I can work on my own for a while."

"Great. Thank you. I don't seem to get enough time these days to look after it properly."

"Maybe I can help," Maggie said.

Olivia's face brightened. "Would you? That would be fantastic. We've been so busy preparing everything for the tourist season, an extra pair of hands would be great."

"Yes, I'd love to, but I'll need to brush up on my gardening skills. It's been a while."

"Oh, I'm sure you'll be fine, but I can give you a run-down of what we're growing if you'd like."

"I'd like that, but no hurry. I'm sure I can tell the weeds from the vegetables."

"Yes, that's not too hard." Olivia chuckled as she returned to mulching.

As Maggie slipped on a pair of gloves and started pulling weeds, she wondered if perhaps Serena might also be interested in helping. It would be something different for her, although she probably wouldn't want to get her hands dirty. She took after Cliff in that regard, but there was no harm in asking.

But what if she left? Maggie grimaced as anxiety began to weigh her down again. She'd just promised Olivia she'd help, but what if she couldn't fulfill that promise? Perhaps she shouldn't have been so quick to offer.

The gate swung open and the children stumbled down the narrow path to where Olivia was mulching the beans. Tears streamed down their cheeks.

Straightening, Olivia folded her arms and asked what had happened.

"Issie pushed me over," three-year-old Will sobbed, looking at his sister with a narrowed glare.

"Did you, Isobel?"

"No. Harriet was chasing me and I ran into Willie by accident."

"A chook was chasing you?"

She nodded.

"Are you sure about that?"

"Yes…"

"You weren't doing anything to upset it?"

"She was," Will said. "She was chasing them around."

Olivia turned to Isobel. "Were you?"

Isobel's bottom lip quivered as she nodded. "Yes."

Maggie chuckled to herself. She couldn't help it.

Olivia spoke sternly. "Isobel, you owe Will an apology. And I've told you not to chase the chooks. They'll stop laying eggs if you do."

Nodding, Isobel turned to Will and wiped her cheeks. "I'm sorry, Willie."

"It's okay," he said, reaching out to give her a hug.

Maggie's heart warmed as she watched the pair, and all of a sudden, a longing to see her own grandchildren filled her. Little Chloe was still tiny, but Sebastian would love it out here. She could picture him running around with Will and Isobel, having a ball. As long as they didn't chase the chooks. Maybe Jeremy and Emma could come for a visit when the rain stopped. It was funny, because until this week, the reality of living so far from them hadn't truly sunk in. But she no longer lived close by, and although she could Facetime with them, she couldn't cuddle them whenever she wanted, and that only made her miss them more.

But she could give Serena a hug.

As Olivia removed her gloves and shepherded the children through the gate, Maggie followed. "I hope you don't mind, Olivia, but I need to see Serena. I'll do some more weeding a little later if that's okay."

"That's not a problem at all. I think she's still on the verandah. Frank was with her earlier."

"Yes, he said he'd try to see her."

"She's not doing too well, is she?"

"No. But I have hope."

"We're all praying for her."

Maggie smiled. "Thank you. That means so much."

When they reached the house, Olivia paused. "I think we'll go in the back way. The kids have got muddy feet."

"Okay. I'll catch you later."

"Sure." Olivia began walking, but then stopped and turned. "Why don't you join us for lunch today since the men are all out?"

Maggie smiled. "That would be nice. Thank you."

"Good. I'll let Janella know."

"Thanks." Maggie stood and watched until the trio headed around the side of the house, Isobel and Will seemingly having forgotten their spat as they skipped along either side of their mother. It wasn't what she'd planned, but lunch with the girls might be just what she needed. And it might even be what Serena needed.

CHAPTER 10

Maggie stood with her hands on her hips. Serena wasn't on the verandah. In the past week, she had been glued to the old cane rocking chair on the verandah, doing nothing other than staring into the distance. She hadn't been reading. She hadn't been talking. She'd just sat and stared, and it grieved Maggie greatly. That was why she'd brought her book with her. She needed to do something while she sat with Serena, especially since she wasn't talking. But now, she wasn't here.

She must be in her room—that was the most obvious place to look. Maggie headed back to the main entrance and walked quietly down the hallway, pausing outside the guest room where Serena was staying. She knocked softly and called out.

No answer. She knocked again, this time, a little louder, but there was still no answer. She opened the door just enough to see that Serena wasn't there. It was strange, but somehow promising, since it meant she was doing something other than sitting or sleeping. But where could she be? Perhaps Janella would know.

The aroma of freshly baked bread wafted from the kitchen, so Maggie headed in that direction. As she poked her head around the corner, she half expected to see Serena sitting on a stool, but only Janella and Sasha were there.

"Hey Maggie, come in," Janella said, a friendly smile on her round face. "I've just made coffee. Would you like one?"

"That's kind of you, but I'm actually looking for Serena. Have you seen her? She's not on the verandah or in her room."

Janella's smile widened. "Yes. She came and grabbed an apple a while ago and said she was going for a walk. You could have knocked me over with a feather."

Maggie sat on a stool, almost in a daze. "I don't believe it."

"I didn't either, but there was something different about her. She seemed to have more spirit. I'm thinking she's turned a corner."

Tears pricked Maggie's eyes as hope filled her heart. "That would be wonderful if it's true."

Janella nodded. "Yes, it would. Now, let me get you that coffee."

"Thank you. I think I need it now." Maggie smiled as she dabbed her eyes and silently thanked God for the encouragement she so desperately needed.

∽

SERENA HAD CHOSEN the path that led into the bushland in preference to the one that led to the lagoon and log cabin or the one that led to the workshops and open grazing land, figuring no one would be in the bush since everyone was working. She needed time to think about what she would do. After Frank's challenge, she felt the need to take action, but didn't know what that should be.

Although the idea of staying at Goddard Downs appealed, would she be hiding from the world if she did? It would be easy. She'd settle into a routine of sorts, and she'd never have to see anyone other than those who lived there. And they'd all been kind to her. Too kind. Just like David.

She let out a deep sigh as she slowed her pace and gazed around. The bushland was peaceful, even with the sound of cicadas and the occasional caw from a crow breaking the silence. But what would staying achieve? This wasn't her home. Her home was in Darwin, where her friends were. Where her job was. But could she return and expect everything to be the same? People would stare. She wouldn't be able to walk down the street or go for a coffee without people turning from her, repulsed. It had already happened. She'd noticed the looks, the glances, the turning away when her scarf had slipped. The thought crossed her mind that she could wear a hijab like the Muslim women did, but she quickly cast that thought aside. Although she'd let her Christian faith slip, wearing a hijab would be hypocritical and inappropriate.

As she walked, twigs broke beneath her feet and she took extra care not to trip. Finally, reaching the edge of the bushland, a majestic vista opened before her. In the distance, shimmering in a heat haze, were the ancient rock formations and dark, jagged outlines of the Mirima Ranges. In between, savannah plains stretched to the left and right as far as the eye could see.

Her gaze caught on a white-tailed eagle soaring over the plains, and once again she thought how wonderful it would be to have wings to fly far away. But she was jumping from thought to feeling like a child playing hopscotch on the playground. The question she had to answer was whether she wanted to live in isolation, or if she wanted to rise above what others thought and regain at least some semblance of her previous life.

Silence wrapped itself around her and brought a little calmness to her soul as she took in the magical vista. Easing herself onto a rock, she took the apple from her pocket. Biting through the skin into the sweet flesh made her think of that verse she'd recalled that morning. Deep down, she knew it didn't matter what she looked like, but would she ever be brave enough to face the world and not let it worry her? And what about what was going on inside her? The way she'd treated David… Since arriving in Paris to be by her side, he'd gone above and beyond to care for her. It might have been partly out of guilt, but he hadn't deserved to be treated with a cold shoulder and snide remarks. And now he was gone. After the words she'd said to him, she doubted he'd ever want to see her again. Despite everything she'd said, that thought filled her with deep sadness and a longing to be held by him.

It had been her who'd stopped their relationship from progressing. She hadn't wanted to be tied down, but perhaps she'd been wrong. Not all relationships ended badly. David was nothing like her father. He was kind, caring, considerate, and handsome. But he was needy. And that's what she didn't like. She didn't like needy. It would never work while he was needy.

All the same, she hoped he'd stay safe while fighting those fires. He'd been a hero on several previous occasions when battling huge fire fronts. He'd even been commended for his efforts. But it was guilt that drove him. She sensed he wouldn't let go until he lost his life saving another. And that was stupid. What use was a dead firefighter? She finished her apple and stood. No, she needed to forget about him.

As she strolled back along the track, she made her decision.

CHAPTER 11

After helping Janella with the lunch preparation, Maggie was setting the table when Serena walked in. Like Janella had said, there was something different about her. Her head was held a little higher, her shoulders set a little squarer, her back a little straighter. Maggie paused what she was doing and smiled. "How was your walk, sweetheart?"

Serena rubbed the back of her neck and rolled her shoulders. "It was okay."

Maggie held her gaze. She knew her daughter and sensed she was holding something back. Perhaps she didn't want to talk in front of Janella. She lowered her voice. "Would you like to chat?"

Serena nodded.

"Let's go outside." She turned to Janella and said they'd be back soon, and then slipped her arm around Serena's waist and walked with her out the door and onto the verandah. A bank of thick, dark clouds was rapidly approaching from the east, accompanied by rumbles of thunder. The afternoon storm was coming early today. Maggie prayed Frank and the boys would find shelter and stay safe, although not many of the recent storms had been violent and they mostly didn't last long, just long enough to cool the air for a short while. "Looks like you made it back just in time." She nodded towards the cloud bank.

"Yes, I didn't see it coming."

Maggie sat on a recliner. "Like what happened with the blast."

"Yes. I didn't see that coming either."

Maggie squeezed Serena's hand. "I wish I could wave a magic wand and change it back to how it was before."

"It's okay, Mum. Somehow, I'll survive. I'm slowly coming to terms with it, although I doubt I'll ever get used to this." She raised her hand to her cheek and winced. "But I have to live with it. I don't have a choice."

"It's going to take time, sweetheart. So, have you decided what you'll do?"

"I have. As much as I like it here, and everybody has been kind and accommodating, I'm going to go back to Darwin. If I stay, I'll only be treading water."

"I thought you might decide that." Maggie drew a breath. "Frank and I will go with you."

"I want to go on my own." Serena spoke with quiet firmness in her voice.

"But—"

"I'll be fine, Mum. I know you only want to help, but I need to find my own way."

"When…when do you want to go?"

"As soon as I can."

"Oh." Maggie gulped. "You won't stay and go on the cattle drive?"

"No. I thought about it, but I want to go home."

"Surely you need someone with you now that David's not there."

"I can look after myself. I can get to my doctor's appointments, I can go shopping, I can do pretty much everything I need to do."

"But won't you be lonely?"

"I have friends."

"Of course you do."

"And besides, I need to find out who I am. I can't do that if I'm with people twenty-four seven."

Maggie was about to say they'd give her plenty of space. She still had her own apartment in Darwin, after all, but she sensed she'd already said enough. Instead, she drew a slow breath and said, "I can understand that. After your father left, I went through much the same type of thing. Everyone thought I needed to be busy to get my mind off him, but what I actually needed was time to process it all and find out who I was when I wasn't Mrs. Cliff Donovan. So, yes, I can understand how you feel. But during that time, I also discovered that talking with others who'd been through a similar experience and come out the other side was helpful."

"There aren't many people who've been through this." Serena raised a hand to her cheek again.

"No, but there are probably more than you think. Turia Pitt, for one." Turia, a beautiful young woman, had suffered catastrophic burns when she and several other competitors in an ultra-marathon race had been trapped by a fire in a gorge not far from Goddard Downs several years earlier. Now she was a motivational speaker and an inspiration to many.

"I DOUBT she'd speak with me."

"You never know, she might, but I'm sure you'll find someone in Darwin, either way."

"I guess I could ask at the Burns Unit."

"That's probably a good idea. In fact, they might even have a support group."

"I'm not sure I want that."

Maggie shrugged. "There's no harm in finding out."

"I guess not. But anyway, I'd like to leave as soon as possible. When do you think that could happen?"

"Frank and I are flying to Kununurra tomorrow afternoon. You can come with us."

Serena's face brightened. "That'd be great. I'll check the flights to Darwin."

"I think there's only one a day and it's in the morning, so you might need to stay overnight. We were planning on staying with Frank's sister and brother-in-law. I'm sure you'd be welcome."

"If that's the only option, I guess I'll take it. Why are you going to town? Anything special?"

Maggie nodded. "We're going to church on Sunday morning."

"Wow. That's a big effort just to go to church."

"I know, but I've been missing the fellowship. We're going to go as often as we can."

Neither spoke again for a few moments, before Serena said,

"Why do you think God allowed this to happen to me?" Tears welled in her eyes.

Maggie shifted closer and squeezed her hand while her heart broke for her daughter. "I don't know, sweetheart, but I'm sure He's got something good planned for you."

"I'm not sure about that. We're not on speaking terms at the moment."

Maggie knew that, and it grieved her, but she had hope that one day soon that would change. "Perhaps not, but His arms are open wide, waiting for You to step into them."

Serena shrugged her shoulders as if she were shrugging the words away. Maggie wasn't sure why Serena had walked away from her faith. She guessed it was the pull of the world, but she knew that God wouldn't give up on her. He'd keep knocking on the door of her heart until she let Him in. He was relentless in His love for His children, and although He didn't cause it, He could use her scarring and a life stripped bare to grab her attention. There were worse things in life than a scarred face, like an eternity spent without Him. Sometimes, it took the loss of things that were considered important to realise they held no importance at all.

Janella poked her head around the corner, glancing between the two of them. "Sorry to interrupt, but lunch is ready if you'd like to join us."

Maggie smiled. "Thanks. We'll be there in a jiffy."

Janella gave a nod and disappeared inside.

"So, will you break the news about leaving now or later?" Maggie asked.

"Since I've made up my mind, I may as well tell them now."

"As long as you're sure."

"I am. And Mum, don't worry about me. I'll be okay."

Maggie reached out and squeezed her hand again. "I know you will, sweetheart. You're a strong girl, but don't be so strong you isolate yourself from everyone. There's real benefit in community."

"I know. I just need time to get there."

"Okay. How about giving me a hug?" Maggie stood and held her arms out.

Serena rose and walked into them. "Thanks for being such a wonderful mum. I love you." Her voice hitched.

Tears pricked Maggie's eyes as she gently hugged her daughter. "I love you, too, sweetheart. I'm so proud of you. But now, let's go and get lunch before we both burst into tears."

Serena sniffed. "Good idea. That bread of Janella's smells so good."

"I know. I'll have to learn how to bake it."

"You? Bake bread? I'd like to see that!"

Maggie hooked her arm through Serena's as they headed inside. "And just what are you saying?"

Serena chuckled. "Nothing."

"Oh yes, you are! I can cook."

"Sure you can."

"Serena…"

"I'm only joking, Mum. You're a great cook." Serena gave her a wink.

Maggie couldn't help herself. She chuckled along with Serena and it felt good. Almost like old times, when neither had a care in the world.

The storm broke as they sat down to lunch, a simple affair —roast beef salad served with crusty bread. Serena broke her news not long after Olivia gave thanks and they'd all begun eating.

After she told them, Olivia said she'd be sorry to see her go.

"You'll be welcome here at any time," Janella added.

"Thanks." Serena smiled gratefully at the two women. "I've really appreciated your hospitality. It's a great place, but I need to go home."

A little later, while they were drinking coffee, Maggie broached the other topics she'd discussed with Frank the night before. She offered her help with the eco tents, which was gladly accepted, and she also mentioned the possible get-together with the other cattle station owners in the area.

"We used to do that once or twice a year when Mum was alive," Olivia said, a wistful tone to her voice.

"They were a lot of fun," Janella added.

"Did you always have them here?" Maggie asked.

Cradling her coffee mug, Janella leaned back in her chair. "Mostly, but sometimes we'd go to the other stations. Everyone camped out overnight. We'd have a barbecue followed by a bonfire, and people often stayed up chatting all night."

"It's a pity we stopped having them," Olivia added.

"Do you think it's a good idea to start again?" Maggie asked. "I'm willing to help if you do."

"I think it would be good," Olivia said. "Especially now when all the stations are struggling because of the live export ban. It'd be good to connect and support each other."

"Great." Maggie smiled, leaning forward. "Where do we start?"

"You're really eager, aren't you?" Janella chuckled.

Maggie cringed. She hadn't meant to be quite so enthusiastic. "I'm sorry. I guess I'm just trying to feel my way."

"It's fine," Olivia said, reaching out and gently squeezing her hand. "We'll look at the calendar and come up with a few dates, and then we'll call around and send out the invitations."

"Oh. I didn't mean for you to do all the work."

Janella chuckled again. "Don't worry. We won't. We'll leave you to organise everything else."

"Okay..." Maggie swallowed hard. She hadn't quite expected that.

"I'm joking, Maggie," Janella said. "We can do it together."

Relief flooded through her. She wouldn't mind doing it all, but not having been to a gathering like this before, she'd flounder if she had to do the first one all on her own.

After a little more discussion, Maggie helped with the dishes and then had a quiet word with Serena. "Would you like to do some work in the vegetable garden with me this afternoon?"

Serena's brows arched. "Vegetable garden?"

"Yes. I offered to help Olivia with it."

"I know nothing about growing vegetables."

"I know you don't, sweetheart. All we'll be doing is pulling weeds."

"Eeww..."

"It's not that bad, although thanks to the storm it'll probably be muddy."

"I guess I don't have anything else to be doing."

"Great." Smiling, Maggie hooked her arm through Serena's and led her to the veggie patch. These snatched moments with her daughter were precious, especially with Serena's planned return to Darwin, and Maggie silently thanked God for them. At least she'd only be a thousand kilometres away, not halfway around the world as she'd been on and off for the past few years.

"What do you think you'll do when you go back home?" she asked as they walked along together.

Serena shrugged. "I don't know. To be honest, I feel at loose ends. That's why I need time to figure things out."

They reached the veggie patch and Maggie opened the gate, motioning for Serena to go in first.

"Wow. This is huge. I had no idea it was here."

"They grow enough vegetables to feed the entire family," Maggie said proudly.

"I guess I should have explored the property more instead of feeling sorry for myself and doing nothing."

Maggie bit her lip. She couldn't agree more but didn't want to say so. "Perhaps the next time you come to visit we can take you on a full tour."

"Including an overnight cattle drive?" When Serena grinned, Maggie's heart warmed.

"I'm sure that could be arranged," she said, smiling.

"Great. I'll hold you to that." Serena surveyed the garden. "So, where do we start?"

"I was working in the bean patch this morning but didn't get a lot done, so we should continue there. Best put these on." She tossed Serena a pair of gardening gloves.

She caught them and held them up. "Eeww. They're dirty."

"What did you expect? Vegetables grow in soil."

"Maybe I should watch. What if I pick up an infection?"

Maggie grimaced. How had she overlooked that? Serena's

wounds were largely healed but she still needed to take care. "I'm sorry, Serena. I didn't think about that risk."

"It's okay. It's just how it is."

"How about we walk to the lagoon instead? The weeds aren't going anywhere."

"That sounds better. And then we could have a game of chess. I reckon I could beat you now."

"You really think so?" Maggie headed out the gate, followed by Serena.

Serena nodded. "David and I have been playing a lot since we got back from Paris."

Maggie's brow lifted. Had Serena forgotten that she and David were no longer a couple? It certainly sounded that way.

But then her daughter's eyes clouded. "I…I should have said we *were* playing a lot. We're not now. Obviously."

"No. So, do you think you'll get back together?"

Serena shrugged. "Unlikely. He's too needy."

"That can change."

"I'm not so sure. Since the day he showed up in the hospital in Paris, he smothered me. It was way too much and I couldn't handle it."

"Did you talk to him about it?"

She nodded. "He doesn't see that he is."

"He's probably worried about you, that's all."

"You don't know, do you?"

Maggie frowned. "Know what?"

"About the fire when he was young."

"No." Maggie's brows scrunched.

Serena blew out a breath. "Let me tell you."

"I'm all ears."

Maggie was gobsmacked. She'd always known David had a story but had no idea he'd lost his mother and siblings in a fire. "So, he's suffering survivor's guilt?"

Serena nodded. "And that's why he takes so many risks when he's fighting fires."

"That makes sense now."

"I can't live with him like he is. He's obsessed. When he saw my burns, it was almost like a switch went off in him and his entire focus was on me. I can't handle that."

"Has he talked to anyone about his issues?"

"Like a psychologist?"

Maggie nodded.

"I suggested he see one, but he wasn't interested."

"Maybe Frank can talk with David when he comes back. He's great at discussing things like that, even though he's not trained."

"*If* he comes back."

"Don't talk like that, sweetheart. Of course he will."

"You didn't see him when I broke it off."

"You're right. I didn't. Was he really angry?"

"That's an understatement."

"Oh."

They reached the cabin, and Maggie suggested a cup of tea while they played chess.

"Sounds good," Serena smiled. "Do you need a hand?"

"Thanks, but why don't you walk to the lagoon while I make it?"

"I might do that. Thanks." Serena smiled again and took the path that led to the water.

While Maggie waited for the kettle to boil, she watched her

daughter through the window. So many emotions were flowing through her, but mostly joy. If she could have fixed Serena's scars, she would have, but that was impossible. Serena would need to learn to live with them, as she'd admitted, but Maggie also sensed a shifting in her daughter's heart, and that gave her hope. *Lord, be with my precious girl. Help her to navigate her way through this and find her way back to You.*

CHAPTER 12

Two mornings later, Serena sat in a small plane headed for Darwin. She was used to flying and had flown in aircraft of all sizes in her role as a reporter, but right now, she felt queasy. Maybe it was simply because the flight was full and she was wedged between the window and an overweight aboriginal woman. Whatever it was, her hands were clammy, her breaths were short, and her stomach churned. If the plane didn't take off very soon, she had no doubt she would vomit.

"Are you alright, love?" the woman asked in a kindly voice.

Serena nodded. "Just a little queasy, that's all."

"First time in the air?"

"No. I'm not sure what it is." Her scarf had slipped, and although her scarred cheek was on the side furthest from the woman, she adjusted it and pulled it tighter.

"Maybe you're pregnant," the woman said brightly, as if being pregnant was something to be happy about.

Serena shook her head vehemently. "I don't think so."

"Oh well. If you want to swap seats, let me know."

Serena offered a cursory smile. "Thank you."

But it was too late to swap seats, even if she wanted to. As the plane began taxiing down the runway and lifted into the air, Serena leaned back against the seat and closed her eyes. The nausea had eased a little, but the woman's words rang in her ears. *Maybe you're pregnant...*

No. The doctors had said her whole body had suffered a shock and that her menstrual cycle might take time to return to normal. Her missed periods were simply that. She wasn't pregnant. Couldn't be. Didn't want to be. But the possibility haunted her for the remainder of the two-hour flight and she found it almost impossible to steady her erratic pulse. *What if she was?*

∼

MAGGIE SMILED at Frank as they walked into the small chapel behind Sarah and Michael, or Mick, as he'd insisted she call him. Last night, staying with Frank's sister and brother-in-law in their home along with Serena, she'd seen a different side to this balding, slightly rotund, jolly man. On previous occasions when they'd briefly met, he'd been polite and reserved, but last night, he'd been the perfect host. Maybe it was because Serena was with them, Maggie wasn't sure, but he'd been attentive and engaging as they sat outside on the verandah and chatted for hours while sipping cool drinks and enjoying Sarah's home-baked goodies. Even Serena had joined in, which surprised Maggie.

Mick had been a long-distance truck driver before he retired and had many tales to tell. Like the time when he, along with fifty other truck drivers, had gotten together and transported two-and-a-half-thousand bales of hay three-thousand kilometres across the country to help farmers on the east coast who were suffering in the drought. The story had brought tears to Maggie's eyes. Serena also shared a story of a similar kindness she'd reported on in England when a group of volunteers rode from Land's End in the south of England to John o'Groats in the north of Scotland to raise awareness and much needed funds to build a shelter for the homeless in London's West End. To make her reporting more authentic, she'd ridden part of the way herself. Humbled by the generosity of the people she met, she'd been challenged to practice random acts of kindness since then. Maggie hadn't known that, but it made her proud.

She was also glad she and Frank had made the effort to come to church. Her only regret was that Serena wasn't with them. Saying goodbye at the airport had been hard. Harder than expected. Her mother's heart wanted to wrap Serena in a big, warm hug and protect her from the world and assure her that everything would be all right, but she couldn't do that. Serena had to take responsibility for her life. Make her own choices and decisions. But whatever path she took, Maggie would pray for her. Maybe it would take years for her to return to her faith. She hoped it would be sooner than that, but she wouldn't give up hope. Deep inside Serena was a God-shaped vacuum waiting to be filled. Until she surrendered her life to Him, she would never experience the true peace that came only from a right relationship with her creator. As

Maggie sat in the pew beside Frank and readied herself for worship, she sent up a prayer for her daughter.

And then the service began. The congregation wasn't large. Less than fifty worshippers stood to sing the first hymn, amongst them, a number of aboriginals and islanders who sang with gusto. Maggie envied those who could outwardly express their gratitude and heart-felt joy to God while worshipping. Having been raised in a more traditional church, and of course, being married to Cliff for all those years, it had been frowned upon to display emotion in church, but sometimes she wished she could simply lose herself in the moment and feel free enough to raise her hands like some of those around her were doing. Maybe one day, but right now, she closed her eyes and sang. God knew her heart, and she knew the words.

Crown Him with many crowns,
The Lamb upon His throne;
Hark! how the heavenly anthem drowns
All music but its own:
Awake, my soul, and sing
Of Him who died for thee,
And hail Him as thy matchless King
Through all eternity.

Crown Him the Lord of life
Who triumphed o'er the grave,
And rose victorious in the strife

For those He came to save;
His glories now we sing
Who died, and rose on high.
Who died, eternal life to bring
And lives that death may die.

Pastor Ned Thomson was an older man with greying hair and a salt and pepper stubbly beard. He welcomed everyone to the service and gave a special welcome to her and Frank, having officiated at their wedding. Maggie's cheeks warmed as everyone turned towards them and smiled. Frank squeezed her hand. He knew she was uncomfortable being the centre of attention, although that quickly changed as Pastor Ned gave the Bible reading from Romans chapter eight, verses thirty-five to thirty-nine.

"Who shall separate us from the love of Christ? Shall trouble or hardship or persecution or famine or nakedness or danger or sword? As it is written: "For your sake we face death all day long; we are considered as sheep to be slaughtered.

"No, in all these things we are more than conquerors through Him who loved us. For I am convinced that neither death nor life, neither angels nor demons, neither the present nor the future, nor any powers, neither height nor depth, nor anything else in all creation, will be able to separate us from the love of God that is in Christ Jesus our Lord."

He looked up and paused before saying quietly, "Will you pray with me?" Bowing his head, he began. "Our dear Lord and Heavenly Father, we humbly bow before You now with gratitude in our hearts for the assurance we have in You. Not one of us knows what tomorrow will bring, but as believers in an almighty God, we can join with Paul and state with assurance that we are more than conquerors, whatever comes our way. Nothing can separate us from Your love, dear Lord. Not famine, nor death, nor war, nor sickness. No, in all these things, Your love will sustain us and we can face trials and tribulations with peace in our hearts. Help us to look up at all times. To trust in Your unfailing love.

"And Lord, right now we pray for those suffering because of the fires down south. Many have lost their homes. Some, their loved ones. We pray that You will provide comfort, and that in this time of loss and heartache, many will seek You. Watch over our firefighters as they battle these dangerous fires. Keep them safe, dear Lord. In Jesus' precious name, we pray. Amen."

Maggie offered her own prayer for David before raising her head. Just that morning, before they'd left, there'd been a news update advising that two firefighters had been badly injured and rushed to the hospital. No names had been mentioned, and she assumed David wasn't one of them, but she didn't know that for sure. Serena had refused to call him, but now Maggie felt the urge to at least send a message and let him know that she and Frank were praying.

The pastor's message was relatively short but to the point as he expanded on the Bible passage he'd read, and by the time the service ended, Maggie felt uplifted and encouraged and determined to keep her eyes and focus on Jesus and to trust Him with all aspects of her life.

At the door, Pastor Ned greeted them warmly as he shook their hands. "It's great to see you both. Looks like married life is suiting you." He grinned as his gaze shifted between them.

Maggie glanced at Frank as he slipped his arm across her shoulders and gave her a squeeze. "It sure is. Good service, by the way. I'm glad we came."

"Thank you. And I'm glad you did, too. How's your daughter, Maggie?"

"On a plane to Darwin as we speak."

"And her partner? Sorry, ex-partner."

"Fighting the fires down south."

"Oh. Let me know if you need any support."

Maggie smiled. "Thank you. I appreciate that."

"You're welcome." He smiled as he extended his hands to the couple following behind.

They walked outside into the heat of the day. Sarah and Mick were waiting for them at the front of the church, but Mrs. Mary, Frank and Sarah's elderly mother, wasn't with them.

"Where's your mum?" Maggie asked, looking around.

Sarah chuckled. "Chatting with her friends. We always have to wait for her."

Maggie wasn't surprised. Mrs. Mary was a character and an inspiration to many, even at ninety-one.

"Did you want to get going or have you got time for a quick lunch?" Sarah asked.

Maggie looked to Frank and shrugged. "What time do we need to leave?"

"Two-ish. I'd like to get home before the storm hits." He checked his watch. "It's only midday, so we've got time for lunch. How about we go out somewhere? Our treat."

Sarah's face lit up. "That would be nice. I wouldn't mind trying that new café on Argyle Road."

"Wivanhoe, you mean?" Mick asked.

"Yes, that's the one."

"Sounds fine to me," Frank said. "All we need now is to find our mother."

Sarah laughed. "I'll see if I can drag her away. I'll try not to be long."

Maggie stood beside Frank while they waited. He and Mick began chatting, and she thought she might use the time to send a message to David. Not that he'd probably see it until later since he was most likely in the thick of things, but he was on her mind. Just because he and Serena had broken up didn't mean she couldn't have any contact with him. She liked the man, and now that she knew about his past, she felt a greater need to help him, even if Serena didn't.

She pulled out her phone and saw that Jeremy had called. She hadn't heard it ring because she'd had it on silent during the service. She thought it a strange time for him to call since he would normally also be in church on a Sunday morning. Something must have happened. Immediate panic welled within her until she remembered the morning's message. *Lord, I'm sorry. Calm my spirit. I trust You, regardless of what may have happened. You're in control.* But as she listened to the voice message, she felt the blood drain from her face. *Mum, Jeremy here. Calling to let you know that the girl passed away this morning and Dad's being charged with manslaughter. He's not doing too well. Will you pray for him?*

She gripped Frank's arm. Although Cliff irritated her immensely and he'd only brought this on himself, she couldn't help but feel for him and for the girl's family. They'd all hoped and prayed she'd survive. Cliff would be a mess. He'd be facing jail for sure, and it would destroy him.

"What's up, love?" Frank asked, his brows drawn together.

"It's Cliff. The girl he hit died this morning."

"Oh. That's terrible. Is there anything we should do?"

She shook her head. "Jeremy left a message asking us to pray, but I think I should call him back."

"Go ahead. Take as long as you need."

"Thanks." She stepped away and made the call. He answered on the first ring. "Mum…" His voice faltered. "Sorry, I'm just coming to grips with it."

"It's okay," she said. "How's he doing?"

"As you'd expect. He's a mess."

"You're with him now?"

"Yes."

"Is he in custody?"

"No. I'm at his apartment. He'll be facing court again tomorrow."

"Serena's on her way home and, in fact, she should be landing about now, although I doubt she'll be of any help, but she should know. Would you like me to tell her, or will you?"

"I'll call her. You don't need to do anything, Mum. He's not your problem anymore."

"I know, but he shouldn't be yours, either. You've got your own family to care for."

"They're okay. Emma told me to do whatever I need to. She said I should stay with him to make sure he doesn't do anything stupid."

"That will be fun for you."

"Yep. The media are outside already."

"Of course they are. What about Mandy? Have you spoken to her?" Mandy was Cliff's second wife, the one he'd had an affair with while still married to Maggie.

"Yes. She doesn't want anything to do with him."

"That doesn't surprise me. Are you sure there's nothing I can do?"

"Pray. The girl's parents are distraught, as you can imagine. It's a sad situation all round."

"Are you okay, Jeremy?"

"Yes. I'm trusting God will bring something good out of it."

"Well, be assured of my prayers. And let me know if I can do anything to help you."

"I will. And thank you."

"You're welcome. Love you, Jer."

"I love you, too, Mum. Take care."

"Thanks." Maggie ended the call and took a moment to compose herself before re-joining the others. Sarah had returned with Mrs. Mary, and the group of four stood quietly looking in her direction. She drew a slow breath, uttered a short, silent prayer for Cliff and Jeremy, and walked towards them.

Frank extended his hand, and when she took it, he squeezed it and looked deep into her eyes. "Are you okay, my love?"

She nodded. "Yes. It was just a shock, that's all. Jeremy's okay. He's with Cliff now."

"He's a good man," Frank said.

"He is. I'm really proud of him. But I've held us up long enough. Let's go and have lunch, shall we?"

"Are you sure you still want to go?" Sarah asked. "I can make a simple lunch at home if you'd prefer."

"That's kind, but I think it would do us all good to go out."

"So long as you're sure."

"I am."

"Well, we'd better get going. Two o'clock will come around quickly," Sarah said.

"Yes, it will." Maggie gave the best smile she could muster and walked with the group to the car, a Land Cruiser that seated eight. Mick helped Mrs. Mary into the front passenger seat, while Maggie joined Frank and Sarah in the back. She clung to Frank's hand and continued to pray for Jeremy and Cliff, the girl's family, and for Serena as she learned the news about her father. And then she remembered she still hadn't sent David a text.

She unlocked her phone again and began composing a message, but then deleted it and began afresh. *David, Maggie here. You've been on my mind and I wanted to let you know I'm praying for you. I hope you're winning the battle and that you're staying safe. Take care. Love, Maggie xx*

They arrived at the café moments after she hit send. It was a kilometre out of town and part of a farm. As Mick steered the car onto the property, she could see the alfresco seating under a shady canopy of mango trees. A young woman sat on a stool singing as she strummed her guitar, her voice melodious and somewhat comforting. It was a lovely atmosphere and helped Maggie take her mind off everything for a while, although every so often, an image of Cliff, Jeremy, Serena or David flashed through it and her pulse skittered erratically. Each time, she uttered a silent prayer and reminded herself to turn her worries over to God. Peace flowed through her until the next image tried to snatch it away again. It was a constant battle. A war between trust and worry, faith and fear, but she needed to keep her eyes on Jesus because He had it all under His control and she had no need to worry or fear.

CHAPTER 13

When Serena turned her phone off flight mode after arriving at Darwin airport, an alert telling her that Jeremy had called popped up. She thought it strange. Although they were siblings, she and Jeremy weren't in touch often. They were too different. He and Emma were the sugary sweet, perfect couple who'd met at church, dated for two years, probably waited until they were married to be intimate, and then had children. They lived in the suburbs in a nice four-bedroom home with a backyard, a pool and a dog, and they went to church every Sunday. Everything she wasn't, nor aspired to be.

She'd never wanted that kind of life. She loved her career and the buzz that came with it. Travelling and living all over the world. Reporting on events as they unfolded. And then, when she came home, which she did several times a year, David would be waiting and they'd pick up where they left off until she went away again. It suited her fine. All the benefits without the commitment. But that was over. She still didn't understand why he'd pressed her to marry him when he knew that's not what she wanted, but she didn't have time to dwell on that right now. She needed to find out what Jeremy wanted.

He'd left a voice message, so, wedging her phone between her ear and shoulder, she listened while she grabbed her bag from the luggage carousel. As she listened, a chill ran down her spine. Setting her bag on the floor, she quickly checked her newsfeed, and there it was, in black and white.

TEN-YEAR-OLD HIT AND RUN VICTIM, KATIE O'ROURKE, DIES. EX-POLITICIAN, CLIFF DONOVAN, CHARGED WITH MANSLAUGHTER.

But the next headline grabbed her attention before she could thoroughly digest the first.

NEW SOUTH WALES FIRES WORSEN AMIDST CATASTROPHIC CONDITIONS

A wave of nausea hit her. Forcing the bile in her throat down, she headed for a chair and took several deep breaths. This was crazy. Normally she wouldn't have felt sick like this. The words spoken by the woman on the plane drifted through her mind but she quickly sent them packing. She was *not* pregnant. It was simply the news that had made her feel nauseous. *Manslaughter... catastrophic conditions...*

Her head swam. And then she couldn't stop it. Vomit raced up her throat and exploded from her mouth like a spout and landed on the floor, splashing her sandals. Her chest heaved. *No. No more.* But too late. Another wave surged through her. As she leaned forward, someone, a man, handed her a paper bag. "Here, use this."

She grabbed the bag and vomited into it.

Finally, she looked around. Everyone was giving her a wide berth. She didn't blame them. Who wanted to be near someone vomiting? To add to the humiliation, her scarf had slipped and her scarred cheek was in full view.

She closed her eyes again and took some deep breaths. When she opened them, the woman from the plane was beside her, holding out a bottle of water.

Taking it, Serena gave the best smile she could manage, and after wiping her mouth with a tissue, took a sip. The cool water was so good, balm to her raw throat. "Thank you," she said.

A male airport cleaner approached with a mop, a bucket and a handful of paper towels.

"Are you sure you're not pregnant?" the aboriginal woman asked, her dark brown eyes soft but probing.

"No!" Serena's reply was short and dismissive. She hadn't meant it to sound rude, so she quickly apologised. "Sorry. I didn't mean to snap."

"It's okay," the woman said. "Sometimes it takes a while to get used to the idea."

"I'm not pregnant." Serena spoke firmly, holding the woman's gaze until the cleaner, who looked Filipino, arrived. "I'm sorry," Serena said to him, lifting her feet.

"It's my job." He handed Serena some paper towels. "For your shoes."

"Thanks." She smiled and took the towels, and after slipping her sandals off, wiped the mess from them. Instead of putting them back on, she opened her bag and grabbed another pair and wrapped the soiled ones in a towel before closing the bag.

The aboriginal woman sat quietly beside her. It was a little off-putting. What was she waiting for? For Serena to confide as to why the thought of being pregnant made her anxious? If she was, she'd be waiting a long time.

After the cleaner left, Serena adjusted her scarf and stood. "Thanks for the water," she said, giving the woman a short nod.

"You're most welcome, dear. Listen, if you ever want to talk, call me." She held out a business card.

Serena's eyes narrowed but she took the card and gave it a cursory glance. Then her brows lifted. *Evelyn Gooding, Family Planning Counsellor.* No wonder the woman's first thought was that she was pregnant. "Thanks, but I doubt I'll need to."

The woman patted her arm. "Time will tell. Take care." She gave a warm smile and toddled off.

Serena gazed after her. She was tempted to toss the card, but at the last moment tucked it into the back of her purse, in between a plethora of other useless cards. She'd clean it out one day, but not now. She needed to call Jeremy and find out what was happening with their father. And then she might send a text to David. She didn't want to talk with him, but catastrophic conditions didn't bode well, and although they'd broken up, she did still care about him.

Knowing a wall of heat awaited her outside the terminal, she sought a quiet corner inside to make the call, but announcements were blasting over the loudspeaker every few seconds and she couldn't hear herself think. It was impossible. She gave up and headed outside. As expected, it was like walking into a furnace after being in air conditioning. It didn't help that it was the middle of the day with no breeze to speak of. And there were no clouds, so no imminent relief was in sight. She turned to the left and walked until the crowds were behind her. Stopping, she unlocked her phone and speed-dialled Jeremy. He answered almost immediately. "Serena—"

"I got the message. How is he?"

"Not great." Her brother's voice was quiet, solemn.

"Where is he?"

"I've brought him to our house to escape the media. Em's taken the kids to her auntie's."

"Do you want me to come over?" Seeing her father was the last thing she wanted to do, but…

"Up to you. I'll be calling someone to take him away soon if he doesn't settle."

"Like, have him committed?" She blinked.

"Yes."

"Is he really that bad?"

"He's having a breakdown."

She swallowed hard. "I'll come straight away."

"Thank you. That would be great."

"I'll be there as quickly as I can." Ending the call, she hailed a cab and jumped in.

Seated in the back as the taxi driver headed to Jeremy's house in the suburbs, memories of her childhood flitted through Serena's mind. Memories she'd rather not dig up, if she were honest. Growing up, all her friends had thought her dad was wonderful. *Cliff Donovan, family man, politician.* They were so envious of her. But he was anything but a family man. He had no interest in what she and Jeremy were doing unless it suited him. He only watched them play sports so he could have his photo in the paper to be seen supporting them. When they got home, it was as if they didn't exist. She didn't know how her mum had put up with him for so long.

When he was awarded "Father of the Year" when she was twelve, she'd almost puked. He was the most two-faced person she knew.

He'd only flown to Paris to be with her when she was in the hospital so it looked good to his constituents. He might have gotten her a better room and preferential treatment, but he was there for his benefit, not hers. He hadn't sat with her and held her hand like Mum and David had for days on end.

Her shoulders fell. She'd meant to text David. Despite everything, she truly hoped he was okay, although she knew that he'd do anything to save another person's life, even if it put his at risk. Opening her phone, she started composing a message. *I just heard about the conditions down there. Stay safe and don't do anything heroic, okay?* She was about to say something about wanting him to come back in one piece but thought twice about it since he might misconstrue the meaning. She didn't want to give him hope, so she simply ended it, *Serena*. No kisses.

The taxi pulled up outside Jeremy's house. She paid the driver and climbed out. Lowset. Cream brick. Tidy garden. It was almost enough to make her puke again. Drawing a slow breath, she walked up the driveway and wondered what awaited her.

CHAPTER 14

At the rate the fire was barrelling towards the small town of Barrimore, David figured they had less than an hour to save it. It wasn't impossible, but it would be a big ask. A miracle. He hadn't seen too many of those this past week.

"What do you think?" he shouted to Troy, his co-captain as the fire truck bounced along the rough fire trail above the town.

"We'll give it our best." Like him, Troy had come from Darwin and was committed to saving as many properties and lives as possible, but he sometimes held back when David rushed in. Not every firefighter was as gung-ho as him. They didn't need to be.

"Good," he shouted back. Two other trucks followed, and each truck carried six firefighters. Eighteen men against a wall of flame. They could do it. The air was thick with smoke and an ominous glow of red headed their way. There was no escape for the people of this town. The wind had changed direction, the roads were impassable, and they were stuck. Anyone who hadn't heeded the call to leave was doomed unless the fire could be diverted.

They reached the end of the trail and jumped out. The task was to set a fire and have it burn everything between the town and the wall of fire roaring towards it so that when they met, with nothing left to burn, both fires would dissipate. It was a gamble. The wind change had slowed the fire but hadn't stopped it. With a mind of its own, this brute still consumed everything in its path and had already jumped containment lines, destroying property, livestock, and acres of farm and bush land. The fact it hadn't taken anyone's life was a miracle. But if they couldn't stop it now, there was no doubt it would cause casualties. Possibly even their own.

Troy barked instructions to the men who complied without question—there was no time to waste. Half were to douse the narrow line between the town and the ridge with water. The other half were to set and manage the back-burn. The wind was too strong and unpredictable for retardant to be air-dropped, the heat too intense for water to have much impact. They had to treat fire with fire. It was dangerous because the wind could change direction at any time. They all knew that. If it did, their only option would be to get out. Quickly.

David led the team setting the fire. He'd done this before and knew what he was doing. He was good at it. It was even said that he had a sixth sense. Maybe he had, he wasn't sure, but he could read a fire as good as any, probably better. Everyone trusted his instincts, and he hoped they wouldn't let him down this time.

The nine men worked together as a team clearing vegetation on the town side of the line before they poured accelerant from one end to the other. Standing between the two teams, Troy gave the nod. David's team was spread along the line, and on his word, the accelerant was lit and flames danced to life and took off. The extreme heat and tinder dry conditions was all that was needed. The wind did the rest. The new fire whooshed and roared as it took off. They'd done all they could, but would it be enough? *Could it stop the fire?*

With their job done, David and three of his team joined the others. The remaining five stayed to monitor the back-burn and alert the others if it turned.

Grabbing a fire hose, David began dousing the trees and undergrowth with water, but his thoughts were on the town folk who'd stayed to protect their homes. No doubt they'd be out with their garden hoses frantically spraying them, hoping it would be enough, but they had no idea what was coming. They needed to find safety, not stand against a fire that didn't play by any rules. If it broke the containment line, a garden hose would be about as helpful as a kid's shovel in a snowstorm. And his sixth sense was telling him it was coming. It was only a matter of time.

He and the men had been instructed to do everything in their power to stop the fire from reaching the town. *But what if they couldn't?* They needed to get the people to safety. There had to be somewhere they could go. As he called Troy on his hand-held radio and peered through the swirling smoke, he sensed, rather than felt, the wind change. Looking over his shoulder, he froze. The fire was racing towards them. His heart pounded as adrenaline kicked in. They had to get out of there, and quick. But they had to warn the town folk. They couldn't let them perish. "Troy, I'm going down."

"Roger that. I'm right behind you."

Large embers swirled in the ferocious wind as thick, black smoke filled the air and cut visibility. The roar of the approaching fire was like a freight train as it hurtled closer. The edge of the township was a few hundred metres to the west. Could they outrun it? He didn't know, but he'd give it his best.

It was difficult to run in his protective gear, but something ignited within him and drove him forward. Once, he tripped over a boulder and landed on his face. He scrambled to his feet and ran on as if a roaring lion were chasing him. The heat was intense and his throat was parched, but he pushed on, and on.

A house came into view through the smoke and relief flowed through him. He headed straight for the back door and thumped his fist on it. "Anybody here?"

There was no reply. The occupants had either left early or were sheltering. He hurried around the side and then to the front. The house appeared empty. He left it and headed to the next one. The properties were on large lots and the next house was a good hundred metres away, surrounded by towering gum trees that would sizzle and ignite in an instant, sending fireballs into the house. Why people built so close to those trees was beyond him. Didn't they know that the oil in the leaves was highly combustible? He put those thoughts aside as he sprinted to the house. The back deck was on stilts, at least twenty metres above the ground and the house was built into the side of the hill. The owners hadn't given much thought to what would happen if a fire roared up that hill, like it was now.

This brute would consume everything in its path, including the house.

Breathless as he reached it, through the smoke, he could just make out the shape of a man frantically spraying the house with water, yelling to someone inside. Panic had set in.

David approached and called out.

The man turned and peered at him, his eyes wide. He appeared to be in his thirties, although it was hard to tell. Whatever his age, he was about to lose his home, but he and his family would lose their lives if they didn't act swiftly.

"How many are inside?" David shouted.

"Three. My wife and two kids."

"You've got to find shelter. You'll die out here."

"I need to save my house."

"No. You need to save your lives. Put that down. Let's go." He placed his hand firmly on the man's back and directed him to the door. "Where are they?" he asked, pushing it open.

"In the bathroom."

"Have you got blankets?"

"Yes."

"Grab them while I run the bath."

"It's already full."

"Even better." David gave the man a nod of encouragement. At least he'd observed some of the guidelines. He peered through the house to the expansive glass doors that opened onto the deck which David assumed would normally give a panoramic view of the town and surrounding area. Right now, the view was a wall of smoke. Thick, insidious smoke that could choke the life from a person in seconds. "Where's the bathroom?"

"Down the hall to the left."

"Grab the blankets and take them there."

The man hurried off in the opposite direction while David headed down the hall to the bathroom and pushed the door open. A young woman sat on the floor cradling a newborn and a toddler. She looked up as he entered, her dark eyes round and filled with fear. He crouched down and spoke gently. "It's okay. I'll get you to safety." He prayed it wasn't an empty promise.

The man joined them, his arms laden with blankets.

"Put the blankets in the water. We need to saturate them."

The man complied. Within moments, the blankets were sodden and heavy.

David pulled one out and placed it over the woman and children. He then spoke to the man. "Put one over yourself and follow me. Hurry."

He grabbed a blanket for himself and held his arms to the toddler. "I'll take him," he said to the woman.

The toddler cried and clung to his mother.

David addressed the man. "Pick him up."

Although the man seemed to be in a trance, he did what David directed.

David glanced outside. They had minutes. Possibly less. "Do you have a water tank? A bunker of some kind?"

The man nodded. "A tank. Out the back."

"Let's go." He ushered them out the back door. Although he was sweating, the howl of the fire racing up the hill sent chills down his spine.

The man headed for the tank. It was a concrete one.

David overtook the couple and instructed them to huddle

on the far side of it. "Lie face down, cover yourselves with the blankets, and pray." He then threw himself on top of them.

His heart thudded as the fire approached. Despite the saturated blanket, the heat was intensifying by the second. They were going to die. Gas bottles exploded, trees crackled and snapped, and a sickening thud told him that at least part of the house had collapsed. The fire was over them. The heat was unbearable, the smoke, pungent. Hell couldn't be any worse than this. Darkness filled his eyes and his world went blank.

CHAPTER 15

Maggie pushed the plate containing the remains of her caramel tart aside and dabbed her mouth with a napkin. Although she'd enjoyed sharing lunch with Frank, Sarah, Mick and Mrs. Mary under the welcome shade of the mango tree, her thoughts were with Cliff, Jeremy, Serena and David. Not that Serena and David were together anymore, but she couldn't seem to separate the pair in her mind.

Frank slipped his hand into hers under the table and squeezed it while asking if she was ready to leave.

She nodded, although she'd rather be flying to Darwin than to Goddard Downs. She'd only said goodbye to Serena that morning, but things had changed already with the shocking news about Cliff. And Sarah had mentioned over lunch that she'd heard the conditions were worsening in New South Wales. Maggie had discreetly checked her news feed on her phone and discovered that her new sister-in-law was right.

The conditions today were catastrophic with extreme temperatures and wind. The authorities expected several towns to be decimated unless the firefighters could gain the upper hand. David was one of those firefighters, and she knew he'd be in the frontline.

Not that she could do anything to change either of those situations, but she felt the need to be close to her family. To support them. To hug them. All she'd be able to do from Goddard Downs would be to talk with them and pray.

Frank pushed his chair back and stood behind her, his hands gently massaging her shoulders as he said to the others, "It's time we headed off, sorry."

"There's nothing to be sorry about," Sarah said. "It was lovely seeing you both. "We're all finished, anyway." She stood and helped Mrs. Mary from her seat and then they all headed to the car.

Mick dropped them to the private airport, and after hugs all round, Frank and Maggie walked across to the helicopter. Although she quite liked flying, she looked forward to the dry season when the roads would once again be open and they could enjoy a leisurely drive.

They climbed aboard and within moments, Frank received the all-clear to take off and soon they were airborne. Puffy white clouds broke up the blue of the sky, but much darker clouds were brewing on the horizon and were headed their way. They'd only just beaten the afternoon storm.

"I'm not sure we'll get much sight-seeing done today," Frank shouted through his headset, nodding in the direction of the clouds.

Maggie shrugged. "I think I'd rather go home, anyway."

He gave an understanding smile and squeezed her hand. "We'll go another day."

"Yes." She returned his smile and then took in the breathtaking panorama. Savannah plains, framed by dark, jagged outlines of the ancient ridges and rock formations of the Kimberley stretched into the distance. Her eyes found a dirt road snaking through the plains and guessed it was the one leading to Goddard Downs. It stopped when it reached the flooded Ord River but continued on the other side, about a hundred metres across the brown, swirling water. Way too far to risk driving across. While writing Clara Goddard's biography, she'd learned that the early settlers in this remote part of the land had been almost totally isolated for up to six months each year during the wet season. At least she and Frank could fly.

They landed at Goddard Downs half an hour later. Instead of going to the homestead, they headed straight for the cabin. Maggie wasn't sure if the family had heard about Cliff. If they hadn't, she wasn't in any hurry to inform them, but if they had, she didn't want to talk about him, at least until she'd spoken to Jeremy again. Once inside, she made a beeline for the kitchen and put the coffee machine on. As she turned to grab the milk, she collided with Frank. "I thought you were upstairs."

"The bags can wait. I'll take them later. I thought you needed a hug."

Tears pricked her eyes as he stepped closer and wrapped his arms around her. How did he always know what she needed? He was so unlike Cliff in every way, and yet it had been Cliff consuming her thoughts.

She rested her head on Frank's chest and thought once

again how blessed she was. "Thank you. I did need a hug." Extracting herself from his embrace, she grinned as she planted a kiss on his lips. "But now I need coffee."

"So coffee takes a higher priority than I do?" He quirked a brow as he leaned back against the kitchen counter, crossing one ankle over the other and pinning her with his amused gaze.

"I didn't say that," she replied as she poured milk into the frother and turned it on.

"No, you didn't. And coffee sounds great. But what are we going to do after that?"

Completely understanding his meaning, she chuckled. Although in their sixties, they were newlyweds, and Frank was as virile and enthusiastic as a man half his age. "I want to call Jeremy and find out how he's doing. Perhaps call Serena. But then…" She angled her head and grinned. "I could be persuaded to have a Sunday afternoon nap."

"I like the sound of that."

"I thought you might." She finished making the coffee and placed the two mugs on a tray with a couple of small pieces of apple and cinnamon bun Janella had made for them. Not that she needed anything more to eat.

Frank offered to carry the tray. "Where would you like to sit?"

"Outside on the verandah?"

"Sounds good to me. The storm's a little way off yet."

"I don't mind getting a bit wet. And besides, I like watching, as long as it's not too violent."

"It could be a doozy, looking at those clouds."

He was right. They'd only just made it back in time. Black

with a greenish tinge, the clouds blotted the sun out entirely and cast an eerie gloom over the lagoon. A clap of thunder sounded, making Maggie jump. "Do you think we'll get hail?" she asked as she sat on the chair.

"Possibly," Frank replied.

"The vegetable garden will get pummelled."

"Don't worry, the girls will have pulled the covers across, or if they haven't, they'll be doing it now."

"I should go and help." Maggie straightened and set her coffee mug down.

He reached his hand out and stopped her. "No need, love. The girls are more than capable. They do it every time we get a big storm."

"I know." She sighed. That was the problem. The girls were more than capable with everything. "I told Olivia I'd do some work in the garden every day."

"I'm sure she'll appreciate that."

"I hope so. I'd like to lighten her load a bit. And Janella's, too."

"You don't need to prove anything, Maggie."

She knew she didn't, but she needed to be doing something to keep her mind active, especially with the recent events. "I know. But I'm looking forward to helping."

"I know you are. And we'll start organising that get-together this week."

She smiled. "Great. The girls seemed excited when I mentioned it."

"I'm sure they did. It's been too long since we had a shindig."

"A shindig?" She laughed. "What are you thinking we'll be doing at it?"

"Oh, maybe some dancing. I can boogie with the best of them, you know."

Her laughter grew. She knew he could dance, but she'd never seen him boogie. "What's gotten into you today?"

He put an arm around her shoulders, and pulling her close, kissed the side of her head. "Being married to you has knocked twenty years off my life."

"You're such a smooth talker, Frank Goddard."

He chuckled. "Wait until you see me dance."

She leaned against him as the storm approached. A huge gust of wind blasted across the lagoon, followed by heavy drops of rain that splashed onto the edge of the timber deck. She snuggled closer, feeling safe in his arms. It was cosy and dramatic all at once as the wind whipped through the trees and the rain grew heavier. Huddling in the corner of the verandah, the storm unfolded before them. It wasn't long before the hail started. Golf-ball sized pellets pummelled the ground and made a deafening racket on the roof.

Just as quickly as it came, the storm disappeared and the sun broke through the clouds, bright and brilliant making everything look fresh and clean.

"I hope the beans survived," Maggie said as she tucked a lock of stray hair behind her ear.

Frank laughed. "Is that all you can think about?"

"No. They just popped into my mind, that's all." She set the mugs onto the tray and stood. "I'll make those calls, and then maybe it's time for that nap."

His face hitched with a grin. "Great. I'll take the bags upstairs and unpack. I'll be ready and waiting."

She bent down and kissed the top of his head. "I'll try not to be long." Reaching the kitchen, she quickly rinsed the mugs and placed them into the sink. She'd wash them properly later. Frank had said they should get a dishwasher, but she'd told him they didn't need one since it was only the two of them.

She pulled out her phone, and perching on a stool, called Jeremy. It rang so long she was about to leave a voice message when he answered. "Mum. Sorry."

"It's okay. How are you doing?"

He blew out a breath and she imagined him raking his hand across his hair. "Not so good. The doctor's here, and so is Dad's lawyer. And Serena, too. She turned up a while ago."

"I thought she might be there. I'm glad she's with you. But tell me, is your father worse?"

"Yes. He's only just stopped pacing. And he's been muttering and yelling for hours. He's gone crazy, Mum."

She could hear the despair in Jeremy's voice and it tore at her heart. "Are you sure he's not putting it on?"

He hesitated before answering. "I don't think he is, but who knows with Dad."

"I wouldn't put it past him. He'd do anything to stay out of jail. Even feign madness."

"The doctor seems to think he's genuine. I guess time will tell."

"What are they going to do?"

"Admit him."

"Now?"

"Yes."

"Oh, dear." The thought of Cliff being admitted to a mental institution sent shivers up her spine. "How is he handling that?"

"It's like he's not aware. The doctor said they'll give him a sedative if he needs it."

"I guess this means he won't be in court tomorrow."

"That's right. It'll be delayed for sure."

"Hmmm… It makes me wonder."

"Serena thinks he's faking, but I'm not so sure. I really think he's having a breakdown."

"Are you okay, Jer?" she asked, wishing she was there to support him.

"Yes, but it's tiring watching him pace for hours on end."

"You sound exhausted. Don't stay with him for long."

"I'm not allowed to go with him. He'll be placed in a secure ward with limited access."

"I wish I could be there for you."

"It's okay, Mum. Emma will come back once he's gone."

"Good. And what about Serena? Is she okay? Has she heard anything from David?"

"She seems a bit anxious but hasn't said much. I don't think she's heard from him."

"I'm praying he's all right."

"So am I. It's pretty bad down there. Two firefighters are dead and three others are critical. It seems like a whole town got wiped out."

She didn't know that. She hadn't checked her news feed since leaving the café. "I hope he wasn't there."

"Me too. Hey, I've got to go. The ambulance has arrived."

"Okay. I'll call back later. Take care, Jer. Love you. Tell Serena I'll call her soon as well."

"Will do. Love you, Mum."

Maggie closed her phone and took a deep breath as a heavy weight settled in the pit of her stomach. It was senseless to worry, she knew that, but hearing about the firefighters had sent a chill through her bones. Even if David was safe, the two who'd died were someone's sons, someone's husbands, someone's brothers. And they'd given their lives willingly to save another. The ultimate sacrifice. And then there was Cliff, who'd taken a life yet was seemingly trying to avoid the penalty. Anger seethed through her. She shouldn't allow disgust for him to affect her, but he was Jeremy and Serena's father, and his actions affected them, and they were her children and she cared deeply about them. They were involved, even if she wasn't. What a mess he'd gotten himself into.

Frank was waiting upstairs, but what she needed more than anything was comfort from the Lord. She flipped her phone open and found her Bible app. At times like these, reading through the Psalms helped soothe her spirit and helped remind her that God was in control. One of her favourites was Psalm ninety-one, verses one and two. She read the words slowly, silently, allowing them to calm her spirit.

He who dwells in the shelter of the Most High will abide in the shadow of the Almighty. I will say to the Lord, "My refuge and my fortress, my God, in whom I trust."

Closing her phone, she bowed her head and prayed quietly. *Lord, help my soul find rest in You. Let me focus on You and not on all the terrible things that are happening. Lord, speak to Cliff and challenge him. Use this situation to awaken his spirit, to change his heart. And be with David, Lord, I pray. I don't know where he is, or even if he's one of the firefighters who lost their lives, but Lord, I pray that he might be aware of Your presence and that will comfort him. Oh Lord, troubles are everywhere. Help me keep my eyes on Jesus, in whose name I pray. Amen.*

As she raised her head, her lips lifted in a smile. Frank had slipped onto the stool beside her so quietly she hadn't heard him and he was now gazing at her with warm, understanding eyes.

"Are you okay, my love?" he asked gently.

Nodding, she reached for his hand.

CHAPTER 16

Gasping, David sucked in a lungful of smoke-filled air. His head spun, his throat was raw. He tried to get up but fell down. Blinked. The last thing he remembered, the fire was coming and he'd taken shelter. The family... had they survived? His heart pounded. He'd never forgive himself if they hadn't. He heard the baby crying and relief flooded through him. They were alive, thank God.

Covering his face with one hand, he helped the man and woman to sit. The man's eyes were round like marbles in his blackened face. Shellshock. The woman was the same. The toddler clung to the man, sobbing. Rocking back and forth, the woman tried to soothe the baby.

"We survived," David whispered. He coughed. How his throat hurt.

They nodded, tears welling in their eyes. "Thank you."

Metres away, trees were burning and crackling as flames

consumed the branches with an insatiable hunger. But they were safe. *They were safe.*

David reached for his radio and called in.

"A rescue truck's on its way," the controller said after David explained where they were. "Until then, stay put."

"We will. Thank you."

He relayed the message to the couple. The man nodded and then scrambled to his feet, his eyes widening. "The house…it's gone." His chest heaved as tears streamed down his cheeks.

"You can rebuild," David said. "You and your family are alive, that's the main thing."

The man wiped his face. "But—"

"Sit down, Stevie. He's right, we can rebuild." The woman reached a hand to her husband.

In a daze, he nodded and sat.

David had seen it all before, but it still wrenched at his heart. They didn't realise how fortunate they were to have survived. They could have easily died. Oh boy, did he know that. A house could be rebuilt—lives couldn't. Once gone, they were gone. There was no coming back.

The woman put her arm around the man and let him sob into her chest while she rocked him and the two children.

A short while later, a vehicle lumbered up the hill and stopped near the tank. David stood and raised his hand to the two men who jumped out and hurried over to him, the burnt ground crunching under their boots. "Hey. How are you doing?" the older of the pair asked, his gaze travelling over David's body. "Are you hurt?"

"I don't think so."

"That's good to hear. And the family?"

"They seem okay, although they're in shock." David nodded his head in their direction.

"You were very lucky."

He knew that. "Did everyone else make it?"

When the man hesitated, David dreaded what he was about to hear. The man finally replied, "Three dead. Two are fireys. Ten critical."

"Troy?"

"Not sure, mate. They haven't released names. Let's get you out of here." He placed his hand gently on David's back and helped him into the truck and then went back for the family.

The makeshift triage tent was on the edge of the town's showground. The ground was charred and the grandstand in ruins. People, dazed, distraught, and shocked, wandered aimlessly. Their town, including their homes, had been razed to the ground and all that remained were charred memories.

The family was attended to first. Apart from smoke inhalation, they were unharmed and David was commended for his efforts. Others hadn't been quite so fortunate and had suffered burns and severe inhalation. Ambulances were lined up ready to transport the badly injured to the nearest hospital, twenty kilometres away.

After David had been checked and cleared, he began the search for his mates. His Darwin buddies. He found them sitting on the ground in a group, bruised, battered, exhausted, but alive. He sat beside Troy and put an arm around his shoulders. Nobody spoke. There were no words to convey how they felt.

Sometime later, on the return trip to base, David checked his phone. There were two messages, one from Maggie and the other from Serena. Both brought tears to his eyes and made him want to go home. But he couldn't go. Not yet. The fires were blazing out of control, and he had to help stop them. That was his job. He replied to each with a simple, *Thanks. I'm alive and okay.* He had no energy to say anything else.

That night, the dream that had plagued him for years became a nightmare, and he knew that when he returned to Darwin, he needed to find out the truth about the fire that killed his family.

∼

SERENA RECEIVED David's message as the ambulance left with her father to take him to the hospital. Tears pricked her eyes as relief flowed through her—she'd thought he was dead. Although names hadn't been released, she'd steeled herself for the news. Not that it would affect her, or so she'd told herself. But as live images of the fires had been played on the television, she knew that if he died, it would be her fault. *How could she live with that on her conscience?*

Jeremy slid his arm across her shoulders as the ambulance disappeared around the corner. "Are you okay, sis?" he asked quietly.

She shook her head and burst into tears. "No, I'm not."

He wrapped her in his arms. "He'll survive. I don't know how, but somehow, he'll survive."

She nodded. She had no doubt their father would survive. In fact, she had a sneaking suspicion he was faking the breakdown to avoid prison. "It's not Dad. It's David."

Jeremy pulled back, his eyes wide. "He's not—"

She brushed her eyes and sniffed. "He's okay. He's alive."

Jeremy expelled a heavy breath. "I thought for a moment you meant the opposite."

"Sorry. I just got a message from him, that's all. It made me tear up."

"You need to talk with him."

She drew a long breath. "Maybe."

He held her gaze for a good few seconds. "Okay. Whatever. Now, do you want to stay, or would you like me to drive you home?"

"I think I'd like to go home, but I can get a cab."

"I won't hear of it. I'll drop you home and then pick up Emma and the kids. Unless you'd like to see them."

Serena shook her head. "Not now, Jer. Maybe another time?" Although they were totally different, she quite liked Emma, and she loved Sebastian, and little Chloe was such a cute baby, but right now, being around them was the last thing she wanted to be.

"Okay. Come on, let's go." He clapped his hand on her shoulder and walked inside with her to grab her bags.

After Jeremy left her outside her apartment block, she walked inside hesitantly. It had been weeks since she'd been there, and it felt strange to be there alone. David had obviously left in a hurry. Dirty plates were stacked in the sink and crumbs were on the counter. His cycling clothes were on the bathroom floor where he must have stripped them off before showering and dressing. The sight of them made her miss him. Perhaps she'd been too tough on him.

She took her bags into the bedroom to unpack but stopped at the door. The bed was unmade and the room reeked of dirty socks and damp towels. Her stomach convulsed and she sprinted for the toilet, only just making it in time.

After she finished vomiting, she stared at herself in the mirror, a glazed look of despair on her face. Maybe the woman was right. Maybe she *was* pregnant. She pressed her hand over her mouth to stop another wave of vomit. As the urge slowly subsided, she sunk to the floor, drawing her knees to her chin and encircling them with her arms. Tears stung her eyes and trickled down her cheeks. *God, I know we're not on talking terms, but please don't let me be pregnant. Please.*

CHAPTER 17

The first few days back in the apartment, Serena was on a cleaning spree. She had to do something to take her mind off the possibility that she was pregnant. As she emptied cupboards, scrubbed floors and sorted through old files, she desperately tried to convince herself she wasn't, but deep down she knew, and she had no idea what to do about it.

If she told David, he'd expect them to get back together, but she wasn't ready for that. Since coming to be with her in Paris, he'd smothered her, treating her like an invalid who needed constant care and attention. She knew he loved her, but he'd changed. He'd always been caring, and she loved his adventurous spirit, but it was like a switch had flicked in him and he'd become so intense he hadn't left any room for her to be herself. *What would he be like if she were pregnant?* No. She couldn't tell him. Not yet. She needed time to figure it out on her own first.

To do that, she needed to go outside and face the world, but the thought of going out scared her almost as much as the thought of being pregnant. But she needed to do it. Tomorrow. Tomorrow she'd go out. Since she'd returned from Paris, Danny, her manager from the broadcasting station had been asking her to visit her colleagues at the studio. So far, she'd made excuses not to go. But tomorrow, she would.

Having made that decision, she had an early dinner and went to bed, exhausted, having worn herself out cleaning.

THE FOLLOWING MORNING, as the first rays of sunlight filtered in through the blinds, Serena was tempted to stay in bed. What on earth had made her think it was a good idea to go out? She lifted her hand to her cheek as tears formed behind her eyes. There were so many things she'd never take for granted again. Smooth skin for one. As well as her cheek, her left arm had damaged skin that would never return to normal, and her legs and chest also were scarred from the multiple surgeries she'd undergone. She hated the way she looked, and it was evident from the way people stared at her that they did, too. How could she ever live normally again? Pulling the covers over her head, she squeezed her eyes shut and hid from the world. She wouldn't go out today. And maybe not tomorrow. Maybe the day after…

But then her stomach convulsed. Throwing the covers off, she sprinted for the bathroom, and once again only just made it. *How could she be pregnant?* Heaving into the bowl, tears mingling with vomit, she faced the reality that she was indeed carrying a child.

Instead of climbing back into bed, she stepped into the shower and turned the heat up as much as her skin would allow. She took her time, allowing the warm water to wash away her tears and soothe her heart. Having children had never been one of her goals. She'd be a terrible mother, and besides, how could a child love her the way she looked? *How could a child even look at me, period?* There was only one way to be rid of a baby that she knew of, and although she prided herself in being a modern, progressive woman, she'd also been raised in the church and her conscience wouldn't allow her to abort a baby. Like it or not, unless there was some other reason for this sickness, she was going to have a child and needed to come to terms with it.

She turned the water off and dried herself slowly. Normally she avoided looking in the mirror, but today she stepped closer and studied her reflection. She didn't like what she saw. The face looking back wasn't hers—it belonged to some disfigured person she didn't recognise. The person's cheek was red and angry after the heat of the shower. The red would soon fade to a leathery brown, but it would never again look normal.

She opened the jar of special moisturising cream she'd been told to use and began massaging the cream into her skin. The doctor said it would help soften it, but she didn't believe him. Her cheek would never be soft again, but her face did feel better when she used it. Her hair was slowly starting to grow back but it was hard to remember how sleek and smooth it used to be. David said he liked it short, but she didn't. He'd only told her that to make her feel better. Other than wearing a wig, there was little she could do except wait for it to grow back. Perhaps she could colour it. Maybe that would make her feel better.

Child, I love you the way you are...

No. Her jaw tightened. Nobody could love her this way. How could they?

I do...I love you...

Ignoring the stirrings in her heart, she turned from the mirror, quickly dressed in her yoga pants and a clean T-shirt, picked up her phone, and made an appointment at the beauty salon down the road.

Two hours later, she emerged from the salon with pink highlights in her hair, polished nails and rejuvenated feet. The stylist, a young woman who hadn't seemed bothered at all by her scarring, had said the pink suited her and helped take the focus from her cheek. She'd also shown her some clever make-up tips that would also help.

Glancing at her reflection in the window, Serena hardly recognised herself. Lifting her chin, she walked along the pavement, passing cafés and restaurants, fashion shops and florists, avoiding the stares of the people she passed. Although they probably didn't recognise her, most would have seen her on their television screens in the past. Serena Donovan, foreign correspondent for the NABC.

But who was she now? That was the question she asked herself as she reached the waterfront.

It was a lovely, warm day, and with her new hairstyle and make-up and the sun on her back, she felt a little more confident about the future. But then she remembered...her future contained a baby. But she didn't know that for sure. Maybe she wasn't pregnant. She should find out, but she didn't want to. Finding out would make it real, and then she'd have to face the reality of it. No. She didn't want to know. Today she'd pretend she wasn't carrying a child. She'd go and visit Danny. But she couldn't go in her yoga pants and T-shirt, so she turned around and walked briskly back to the apartment and exchanged her casual wear for more appropriate clothing—clothes she hadn't worn since before the blast. White linen pants, a bold pink shirt that matched her hair colour, and heels.

A tiny smile tugged at her face as she appraised herself in the full-length mirror. Maybe Serena Donovan, foreign correspondent, could make a comeback. Her scarred cheek would be a constant reminder to her viewers of the sacrifice she'd made to bring them breaking news from around the world. Hope grew within her. Maybe she could have her old life back. The thought of it sent a warm glow through her, but then, just as quickly as it came, that hope was extinguished, replaced by a sense of despair. She could never have it back if she was pregnant.

Trudging into the kitchen, she opened the fridge and grabbed a can of Coke, one of David's leftovers. The message he'd sent the other night had been brief, but at least she knew he was alive. She hadn't sent him another, but after easing herself onto a stool, she flicked through her news feed to see if there was any mention of him. And there was. The information was from two days ago, but there it was. *David Kramer, firefighter from Darwin, hailed a hero after saving the life of a family in the southern New South Wales township of Barrimore.*

Of course he'd been hailed a hero. That was how he lived his life. All in. Totally focused. He got up when he fell down. He never gave up. He pushed on. And yet he *had* given up. When she told him she wouldn't marry him, he'd walked out. Abandoned her. She hadn't expected that. Sipping the Coke, she pondered. Something had changed inside him, but she didn't know what. He'd always been hesitant to talk about his early childhood. She knew he'd lost his mother and two younger siblings in a house fire when he was four. His father had survived but suffered a breakdown and became an alcoholic, and David had been taken in by his aunt and uncle who raised him as one of their own. She sensed his recent change of behaviour had something to do with memories of those early years. Perhaps her injuries had triggered something deep inside. Perhaps there was more to the fire than he'd told her. She was a journalist. Maybe she could do some digging. She could even start today. Finishing her drink, she slipped off the stool, grabbed her purse, and headed out with a spring to her step.

She hailed a cab and gave the address of the station. It was lunchtime when she arrived. She hadn't planned it that way, but perhaps it was a good thing since there would be less people to ask her questions, to say how sorry they were.

Outside the entrance to the five-story modern building in downtown Darwin, she hesitated. Was she truly ready to face her colleagues? They'd been so kind and had sent numerous well-wishes, cards and flowers, but they had no real idea of what she'd been through. Seeing the pity in their eyes would bring tears to her own. As she lifted her hand to her cheek, her resolve slipped. Backing away from the door, she turned and ran headlong into Danny.

"Serena! Is that you?" Her boss removed his tinted sunglasses, his gaze sweeping over her. In his late forties, Daniel Coleman was dressed in faded jeans, a button-down shirt rolled to the elbows, and Nike slip-ons. He didn't look like the manager of a broadcasting station. "You look great!" He leaned in and gave her a cautious hug.

"Thanks." Giving him a small smile, she returned his hug.

"Did I miss your visit?"

She shook her head. "I changed my mind and didn't go up."

"Serena. No one's going to stare at you. They'll love seeing you. How about I buy you some lunch and then we can go up together?" Before she could reply, he'd slipped his hand on her waist and pulled her out of the way of the throng of people who'd crossed the road when the lights changed.

As the huddle passed by, she felt claustrophobic. And sick. *No...* she couldn't be sick here. Not on the footpath. Not with all these people around. "I'm sorry, Danny. I need to go home." Her breaths came faster and she thought she was going to faint.

"Serena, what's wrong?"

She shook her head, almost unable to speak. "I feel sick."

"Come inside and sit down." He pushed the door open and held it for her.

She didn't want to go inside, but she did need to sit. He directed her to a plush armchair in the foyer and fetched a cup of water from the drinking fountain. By the time he returned, her breathing had calmed and her stomach had settled. She sipped the water gratefully. "Thank you," she said, offering him another small smile. "I'm not sure what brought that on," she lied.

"It's probably because you've been hiding away for so long."

"Yeah. That's probably it." She took another sip.

"So, now that you feel better, let's grab a bite to eat and have a catch up."

She blew out a breath. She'd rather go home, but since she was here she figured she may as well stay. "Sure," she said. "But can we go somewhere quiet?"

"Whatever you want, my dear." He extended his hand to help her up. She didn't need help, but she took it anyway. It would be rude not to.

"Where would you like to go?" he asked.

She shrugged. "How about Arthur's?" Arthur's wasn't one of the restaurants frequented by the staff of the NABC, even though it was close by. She and colleagues favoured the newer restaurants and cafés at the marina, so they might avoid bumping into anyone she knew by going there.

"Sure. Arthur's is fine. We can duck out the back way."

She smiled at his understanding and walked alongside him, changing sides so her good cheek showed. If he noticed, he didn't say.

"I'm sorry about your dad," he said once they were out of the building. He knew her father, although they weren't exactly friends. More acquaintances than anything.

"Thanks," she replied. "I feel sorrier for the girl and her parents than I do for him, though."

"It's very sad. He should have known better than to be drunk driving."

"Yes, and I think he's faking this breakdown." As soon as she said it, she wished she could retract her words. Danny was the last person she should have confided in. She turned and pleaded with him. "Please don't release that. I shouldn't have said it."

He gave a lopsided grin. "And what do I get in return for withholding that piece of interesting information?"

He was flirting, but somehow she didn't mind. "Nothing," she said, playing along with him for a bit of fun.

His shoulders fell and he looked crestfallen, but she knew he wasn't serious. Danny never took advantage of his position. That was one thing she liked about him. She gave a small chuckle. "Come on, Danny. Do the right thing."

He winked. "Of course I'll keep your secret, Serena. And tell me, how's David?"

A small breath flew from her lips. Why did the mere mention of David's name cause an ache in her heart? "You might as well know—we broke up a few weeks ago."

"No way!"

"It's true." She left it at that. Danny didn't need to know the details, although he'd raised a brow and was obviously curious.

They reached the restaurant and he stood back, letting her enter first. They headed for the tables on the far side that ran alongside the wharf and had a great view across the harbour. After being seated by a waiter who left them with menus after filling their glasses with water, Danny asked what she'd like to eat.

The thought of eating turned her stomach, but she had to get something. "Nothing big, a salad sandwich will do."

"Lost your appetite?" He lowered the menu and studied her over the top of it.

She shrugged. "I'm not that hungry."

"Okay. But I think I'll have the hamburger with the works."

Her stomach seized and she pushed her chair back while covering her mouth with her hand, almost knocking the chair over in a hurry to stand. "Excuse me." Without saying another word, she fled to the bathroom.

Fortunately, no one else was inside. As she heaved into the toilet bowl, she wondered why she'd ever thought eating out was a good idea. After she cleaned herself up, she returned to the table. "Sorry about that."

He studied her intently. "So, how are you really doing, Serena?"

She squirmed under his intense gaze. Direct questions weren't easy to answer, especially when asked by people who knew her well. And Danny did. She toyed with her glass of icy-cold water. He was waiting for an answer. She drew a deep breath and lied. Again. "I'm doing okay."

"Really?" He quirked a brow.

Shrugging, she brushed a tear from her eye and looked away. "No. Not really."

"I know it's none of my business, but do you want to talk about it? Is it David?"

It wasn't any of his business, but all of a sudden she felt like confiding in someone who knew them both. She swung her gaze back to his, swallowing hard before she blurted out, "He asked me to marry him, and I said no."

"Oh."

"And now we're not talking, and he's off fighting those fires."

"You're worried he won't come back?"

She nodded and briefly closed her eyes. She hadn't acknowledged that truth until now, but Danny was right. That's what worried her. That David wouldn't come back. That she'd driven him away and he might die. *And that he'd never know about the baby.*

Their meals arrived and it took all her effort not to vomit again.

"So, what are your plans," Danny asked as he nibbled a chip. "Will you come back to work?"

She took a deep breath. "I don't know. It's too soon to decide."

"You need to be doing something."

"I know. I'm trying to figure out what." She took a tiny bite of her salad sandwich.

"I've got a job that might tempt you back."

Her forehead creased. "What's that?"

"Host of the morning talk-back show."

"Radio?"

He nodded as he bit into his hamburger, unsettling her stomach again.

"I'm not sure that's for me."

"You'd be great at it."

It was something to think about, but being stuck in a broadcasting studio chatting with a bunch of self-opiniated listeners honestly didn't appeal. However, her options were limited. Nobody would seriously consider putting her back in front of a camera.

"I guess I couldn't have my old job back?" She threw it out there as a test, although she already knew what the answer would be.

Leaning back in his chair, he folded his arms and looked her in the eyes. "Serena, I'm sorry…"

She held up her hand. "It's okay. I get it. How long do I have to decide?"

"A week."

"Hmmm…"

He leaned forward. "I'm really sorry for what happened to you, Serena."

"Thanks." She pushed her unfinished sandwich aside and tried to quell her nausea. She was tempted to tell him about her suspected pregnancy, but decided he probably wasn't the right person to confide in, although she knew he'd take it in his stride. No, if she were to tell anyone, it would probably be Jeremy and Emma, although they had enough on their plate already. Maybe a better option would be that woman on the plane. Or her mum. Or David. No, not David. That made her remember what she wanted to ask Danny. "Hey, can you do something for me?"

"Sure. Name it."

"Will you look into the archives and see what you can find out about a house fire that happened in 1989 in Nightcliff?"

"Nineteen eighty-nine?"

"Yes. It was the fire that killed David's mother and his two siblings."

His forehead creased. "What do you want to know about it?"

Toying with her glass, she gazed across the clear blue

waters of Darwin Harbour. "I'm not sure. I just feel that a stew of unwanted memories have been stirred up within David." She swung her gaze back to Danny. "Since this happened," she lifted her hand to her cheek, "he's behaved differently, like a switch flicked in him. He's having trouble sleeping, and he's intense with everything he does. I think the answer lies with what really happened in that fire."

"Okay, I'll see what I can uncover." He smiled. "He's a good guy, Serena. I wouldn't let him get away if I were you."

"Wow. I never thought I'd hear you say that."

He shrugged. "Neither did I, but to look after you the way he did, that was pretty special."

"And that's the problem. He didn't just look after me, he smothered me, like he was trying to justify living."

"Survivor's guilt and all that."

"Yes, but he's almost thirty-five years old. It happened a long time ago."

"Yeah, I guess there's that."

"Anyway, will you look into it for me?"

"Sure, I'll do my best. Now, would you like coffee or shall we head back?"

"Would you mind if I go home and come back another day? All of a sudden I'm feeling really tired."

"No, that's fine. At least we've caught up."

"Thank you." Smiling, she pushed her chair back and stood. As they headed out, her phone beeped. She glanced at it while Danny paid the bill. It was a message from Jeremy asking if she'd like to visit their father with him. It was the last thing she felt like doing, but she figured she probably should. She quickly typed a reply and said she'd meet him at the hospital in half an hour.

Outside the restaurant, Serena thanked Danny and promised she'd think about the job offer. He promised he'd look into the fire. They hugged and then she jumped into a waiting taxi and gave the driver the name of the psychiatric hospital where her father was.

CHAPTER 18

After Serena returned to Darwin, Maggie kept herself busy tending the vegetable patch and planning the 'shindig', as they'd all started calling it, not only to give her something to do, but to keep her from worrying. With Cliff in a psychiatric hospital, David in the midst of fires that weren't easing, and Serena back in Darwin on her own, she had to keep occupied, although prayers for all three were constantly on her lips and her heart.

With the help of Frank and the girls, they'd made a list of neighbours to invite and had started making the calls. Well, she hadn't. Frank and the girls had. But she listened while they chatted and was growing excited about meeting their neighbours. So far, three families had said they could make it, while one, the Clermonts, said they weren't sure if they could leave their property for a whole weekend, but would try to get someone in to tend things.

They had one more call to make, to the folks at Brampton

Downs where she and Frank had celebrated their wedding. Frank was making the call that evening after dinner.

She'd baked his favourite meal of lasagne and was pulling it from the oven when her phone rang. She quickly set the hot dish on a trivet and answered. She already knew it was Serena from the ring tone. "Serena! I was going to call you tonight. How are you doing?" Maggie eased herself onto a stool and looked outside at the stunning sunset.

"I'm fine." But she didn't sound fine. Although her voice was upbeat, it held a slight hitch.

"Are you sure you're okay, sweetheart?" Maggie asked.

"Yes. I had my hair coloured today."

"Oh. That's good. What colour?"

"Pink."

Maggie's eyes widened. "Pink?"

"The stylist suggested it."

"Oh. You'll have to send me a photo."

"Okay." A pause. "I bumped into Danny today. He offered me a job."

"Really? That's great."

"I don't think I'll take it."

"What is the job?"

"Radio talk-back host."

"You don't sound keen about it."

"I'm not."

"You sound a little lost, sweetie."

There was a long pause before Serena replied, and Maggie began wondering what had happened. Worry nibbled at her again and her stomach began churning before she gave her worry to the Lord.

"I don't think I'm ready to go back to work yet."

Maggie released a breath. That's all it was. "I agree. It's probably too soon. There's no hurry to go back." She wanted to ask if Serena had spoken to David, but stopped herself. It was none of her business. "How's Danny?" she asked instead.

"Fine. Same as usual."

Maggie smiled. "He's a nice man."

Silence.

"Tell me, sweetheart, have you spoken to David?" She couldn't help herself.

"No, Mum. We've broken up, remember?"

"Haha." Maggie bit her lip. "Sorry. Yes, I do remember. I was wondering, that was all. I'm missing you, Serena."

Maggie thought she heard a sob. "Serena, are you okay?"

"Yes. I've got to go, Mum. Good talking with you."

"And you. Take care, sweetheart."

"I will."

When the call abruptly came to an end, Maggie remained deep in thought. There was something unusual in her daughter's tone. She couldn't put her finger on it, but something was wrong. She just knew it.

Moments later, Frank's truck pulled up outside and he climbed out. She slipped off the stool and hurried to greet him. Even though she was keeping busy, the days seemed so long when he wasn't there.

A smile lit up his face as she walked towards him. He held out his arms, slipping them around her as he kissed her on the lips. He smelled of hard work and manly sweat, but she didn't care. In the half light, against a horizon of deep orange, her heart swelled with love. As she snuggled against him, her worries over Serena slipped away. For a moment.

"How's your day been, love?" he asked as they walked arm in arm up the stairs.

"Interesting."

"Oh. What happened?" He opened the door for her and then followed her in.

"I just had a call from Serena. She hasn't been herself for some time now, but I sense there's something more going on."

He walked to the fridge and pulled out a jug of water. "She has a lot to deal with right now."

She leaned against the counter and folded her arms. "Yes. Between her depression and lack of self-confidence due to her injury, her father's problems, and David risking his life fighting those fires, her cup is full."

"You could call Jeremy. See if he knows if anything else has upset her since she got back to Darwin." Frank poured himself a large glass of water and drank it all in one go.

She nodded. "I might do that. But let's have dinner first."

"Good idea. I'm ravenous."

She laughed. "Just as well. I made enough lasagne for an army."

He chuckled. "Let me clean up first and I'll set the table. Outside or in?"

"Outside? It's a lovely evening." She grabbed a knife and began slicing some tomatoes for the salad.

"It is. Outside sounds perfect." He came up behind her and slipped his arms around her and nuzzled her neck.

"Frank!" Putting the knife down, she spun around and linked her arms around his neck. As his lips lowered to meet hers and she lost herself in his kiss, she decided that dinner could wait.

~

Serena flopped onto the couch and closed her eyes. She was so tired, and although her body craved sleep, her mind wouldn't stop. It was spinning so hard it was almost out of control.

After visiting their father in the hospital, she was coming to think that he was indeed losing his mind and he wasn't faking his breakdown. Seeing him huddling in a corner on the floor, muttering like a crazed person, had shaken her to the core. Although she didn't hold much respect for him, he was still her father, and it grieved her deeply to see him so troubled.

Perhaps it was that depth of emotion that made her tell Jeremy about her suspected pregnancy. She hadn't meant to tell him—the words just poured out of her mouth as he drove her home. He'd been understandably shocked and was speechless for several moments before he told her she needed to find out for sure. He also said that Emma would go with her to the doctor in the morning.

Serena had grimaced, said it wasn't necessary, but he insisted. "You can't find out news like that on your own, sis. Trust me, you'll want someone with you."

After he left, she felt the desperate need to be hugged by her mum, but her mum was a thousand kilometres away. Instead, she rang her, and listening to her mother's voice made her a little calmer. Until her mum said she missed her. Then she broke down in tears and sobbed uncontrollably for half an hour. *What was happening to her?* She'd lived halfway around the world for months on end and had never been so emotional or needy.

Squeezing her eyes shut, she tried to empty her mind, but the harder she tried, the more it spun. Finally, she swung her feet to the floor and turned the television on. She flicked through the channels, but as she stopped on a news channel that was giving a report on the fire situation down south, she realised it was a mistake. Her thoughts turned immediately to David. Deep down she knew she'd hurt him. He'd been nothing but kind to her over the years, but she'd kept him dangling, saying she wasn't ready to settle down. But perhaps it was more that she was scared of love. Of allowing herself to be vulnerable. Of exposing her innermost thoughts to another. Maybe she had to take a risk and allow herself to be vulnerable. If she truly wanted peace and happiness ever again, maybe she needed to drop her guard.

She picked up her phone and called him.

CHAPTER 19

*D*avid was eating a late dinner after another long, hard day on the front. They were slowly winning the battle, but as soon as one front was controlled, another blaze flared up. It was constant and tiring, and he was bone weary. He and his mates from Darwin had stuck together, and a deeper comradery had formed between them. Trust had grown and friendships had deepened. In particular, he'd gotten to know Troy Barrington better. They'd been work mates before, but now, Troy had become his friend.

It began one night when David was having one of his bad dreams. He'd woken in a lather of sweat to find Troy beside him, looking at him with concern. "Hey, Dave, what's going on?" he asked.

Sitting, David cradled his head in his hands and fought back sobs. He didn't want to cry in front of his mate, but the images had been growing more vivid with each dream, and in this last one, he'd seen something that shocked him to the core. It couldn't be true. It just couldn't.

"Come and have a drink," Troy said.

David got up and followed him to the canteen. Troy grabbed two beers from the fridge and they headed outside. Except for the orange glow on the horizon, the sky was dark. The air was heavy with smoke, but he didn't smell it. It was normal now. They sat at a table with only the glow for light, while the wind whistled through the trees, and he told Troy about his dreams. He wasn't sure why, but he felt the need to talk about them, and Troy was there.

"I think I lit that fire," David said carefully. The very words tore at his heart. Ripped it apart!

"You don't know that for sure," Troy said. "Dreams are strange and usually don't make any sense."

"But it was so real."

"You were only four. Seems impossible that you could have started a house fire."

David drew a long breath and curled a hand behind his neck. "I know. But I need to find out."

"And if you discover that you lit it?"

David shrugged. "At least I'll know, and then maybe I can deal with it."

"I know only one way of dealing with things like this," Troy said.

"Yeah? What's that?"

"Prayer."

"Prayer?"

Troy nodded. "I believe in God. He knows our pain and our

heartache, and He can reach deep within us, heal our memories, and release us from guilt. Can I pray for you?"

It was the last thing David had expected, but somehow it felt right. So, out there in the dark, with his heart exposed, he allowed Troy to pray for him. Tears welled in his eyes as Troy asked God to take the burden from him. To release him from guilt. To fill him with peace. They'd hugged and been firm friends since. The dreams hadn't stopped, but when he woke, he felt a little less burdened. When he got back to Darwin, he would discover the truth about that fire. And Troy said he'd help.

His phone rang as he was finishing his dessert. He knew who it was from the ring tone. Serena. It had been days since he'd sent her a message. Because she hadn't replied, he'd convinced himself he'd never hear from her ever again, so now, his heart leapt. He pushed back his chair, excused himself, and walked away from the noisy canteen.

Drawing a steadying breath, he accepted the call. "Hey, Serena. How are you doing?"

"Not too good." Her voice was softer than usual and lacked the confidence she'd always exhibited. The results of the explosion were evidently still wreaking havoc on her life and his heart went out to her.

"What's wrong, babe?"

She began sobbing.

"Serena?"

"I'm…I'm sorry."

He swallowed hard. "It's okay." Whatever it was she was apologising for, it was okay. He didn't care. "I love you."

She sniffed. "I love you, too. I'm sorry for how I've treated you."

He blinked tears. Her words were a balm to his weary soul. "Oh babe. There's nothing to forgive. You've been through so much."

"But it doesn't excuse my behaviour."

Perhaps not, but what did it matter? They were on speaking terms again, and that's all he cared about. "Where are you?"

"Back home."

"I wish I could be there with you."

She sniffed again. "When will you be back?"

He gazed at the glow on the horizon and his shoulders fell. "I'm not sure. The fires are still bad."

"Are you being careful?"

How did he answer that? He took calculated risks, but sometimes those risks put him in danger. That's what he did. That's what he'd always done. He did it to assuage his guilt. To justify living when his mother and siblings had died. And now… now it would be even worse if he discovered he was responsible for their deaths. But he couldn't tell her that. Instead, he replied, "Of course I'm being careful."

"Good. I've got to go now, I'm sorry. I'll talk to you later."

"Okay. Thanks for calling. I love you."

But she'd disconnected the call and his misgivings about her mental state increased by the second. Something was amiss. He just didn't know what.

CHAPTER 20

The night seemed never-ending. The empty apartment engulfed Serena with dreadful loneliness. She tossed and turned, and at one stage, got up and opened the Bible Frank had given her before she left Goddard Downs. She hadn't opened a Bible since before going to university, but as she flipped through the pages, some of the verses seemed familiar, the words comforting.

She stopped at Philippians four and read the verses slowly. *Be anxious for nothing, but in everything by prayer and supplication, with thanksgiving, let your requests be made known to God; and the peace of God, which surpasses all understanding, will guard your hearts and minds through Christ Jesus.*

But how could she pray when she'd walked away from her faith? *From God?* She'd questioned the beliefs of her childhood and had followed the popular trend of living for herself, of believing that was all there was. But something told her those beliefs were wrong and that God did exist and that life was more than a matter of being born, living three score and ten, and then dying. If that's all there was to life, what was the purpose? *But would God have her back?* Were His arms truly wide open, like Mum had said they were? She'd also said that peace wasn't the result of things going well. It was the presence of God in the middle of trials. It didn't depend on her situation. True peace was about wholeness and being one with God. It was a gift, flowing out of His love for her.

SERENA DIDN'T KNOW if He'd hear her words, but she hoped He'd hear the cry of her heart. She fell to her knees and opened it to Him.

Afterwards, she felt cleansed. Lighter. And she also knew that if she were pregnant, God would be with her and would give her the strength to face whatever lay ahead.

Morning finally came. The day of reckoning. Emma sent a text saying she'd be there at nine. Serena looked at the time—it was almost eight. She'd slept longer than expected. And then she remembered the events of the previous night. It almost seemed surreal. *Had she really gotten down on her knees and prayed?* It seemed like a dream. But then her gaze landed on the Bible on her bed stand, open at Philippians. She picked it up again and reread the verses. As she did, peace filled her and she knew she hadn't imagined it. She lifted a hand to her cheek, hoping that perhaps some miracle had happened in the night as well, but no. The scar still felt rough and raw. And then her stomach churned and she dashed to the bathroom. Nothing had changed, and yet, it had. She had a new confidence that she would survive.

After showering and dressing, she forced herself to eat a piece of toast which she ate while sitting on the balcony. The bay was crystal blue, reflecting the hue of the sky, and for the first time in a long time, she appreciated how beautiful it was. The only thing missing was David. Speaking with him the previous evening had stirred feelings she'd been pushing aside, but his caring voice had slid under her skin and grabbed her heart and she realised how much she loved him. The question was, could she live with him? *Could she live without him?*

The buzzer for the apartment sounded. Emma was here. Serena carried her plate to the kitchen and spoke through the intercom. "I'll be down in a jiffy."

Emma replied that there was no hurry.

Serena cleaned her teeth and quickly applied her make-up, using the tips the stylist had given her. The scars on her cheek were still noticeable, but her pink hair and kohl-rimmed eyes detracted a little from them, or so she hoped. Today, however, that didn't seem quite so important.

Grabbing her purse, she headed out. Emma was standing on the opposite side of the road gazing across the bay, wearing a knee-length, body-hugging summer dress that showed off her plus-size figure. She was only two years older than Serena, but she couldn't be more different. She was still carrying some baby fat that hadn't shifted for months. Serena guessed it might be a permanent fixture. She was alone, as Serena had hoped she would be. As much as she loved her little niece and nephew, today was not the day to have them around.

She crossed the road and called out. Emma turned around and her eyes popped. "Serena! Look at your hair! It's gorgeous." She moved towards her, and after they embraced, she stepped back to take a good look. "Jeremy said it was pink, but I couldn't quite imagine it. You know me. Madame Conservative, and all that."

Serena smiled and thanked her. Emma's light brown hair was pulled back in a messy bun and really could do with some TLC, but Serena knew she didn't care too much about her appearance. She was a jolly soul who seemed happy in her own skin.

"We've got time for a quick drink first, unless you just want to get there," Emma said.

"I think I do. Plus, I'm still feeling a little sick."

Emma chuckled. "I know that feeling. Come on, my car's over here." She held the car beeper out as they approached and then hurried ahead to open the front passenger door. "Sorry about the mess. I meant to clean it before I dropped the kids off to my auntie, but I ran out of time."

Serena glanced in the back. It could certainly do with a clean. It wasn't so much dirty as untidy, with kids' shoes, clothes and toys scattered on the floor and seat. "It's fine," she said as she climbed in. She didn't quite understand how mothers always seemed to have no time for things like cleaning up their car, but she guessed she'd be finding out soon enough. And with that thought, her anxiety returned. The truth was, she didn't want to be a mother. She didn't want that kind of life. Something would need to shift inside her to make her feel comfortable with the notion, and she had no idea how that would happen.

They made small talk on the way to the medical centre, but when Emma parked the car and turned the engine off, she faced Serena and asked how she was feeling.

Serena inhaled slowly and stared at her hands. She was trying to force her mixed emotions into order as the moment of truth neared, but she mostly felt calm, which surprised her. It was probably because she already knew she was pregnant and a shift had begun. She raised her head and met Emma's gaze. "I'm okay."

"Good." Emma reached out and squeezed Serena's hand. "Being pregnant isn't the end of the world. It's an amazing, special time, and I pray that if you are, it will be a real blessing for you."

Serena managed a half smile. That was one of the things that irritated her about Emma. She might be genuine in her faith, but she spoke in words that most people would cringe at, but she didn't seem to notice or care. "Thanks," was all she could say.

They exited the vehicle and walked inside the centre, a large, modern building in the middle of downtown Darwin. Three women wearing dark blue patterned shirts sat behind the semi-circular reception desk. One, a woman who had worked at the clinic for almost as long as Serena had been a patient, looked up and waved them over. "Ah, Serena. I almost didn't recognize you with that hair. It looks good, by the way."

Serena smiled. "Thank you." It seemed her new look was working.

The woman looked at her screen. "You're here to see Dr. Mitchell."

"Yes." Serena nodded.

"Take a seat. Doctor will call you shortly.

"Thank you."

She and Emma found two chairs together on the far side wall. The waiting room was busy. It seemed like everyone in Darwin was seeing the doctor today. The television was on, but the sound was low. Knowing a news update would come on at some time, Serena tried not to watch it, but her gaze was drawn to the screen and thoughts of David drifted back. He should be here with her. Not Emma. *If her pregnancy was confirmed today, would she tell him?* She wasn't sure. Although she loved him, there were a lot of issues for them to work through. They couldn't go back to how it was after they returned from Paris. And depending on what Danny discovered about the fire, there could be even more to resolve. No, she wouldn't tell him. Not yet.

Time passed. Other patients were called in. Finally, it was her turn. "I'll wait here unless you want me to come with you," Emma said.

"Thanks. I'll be okay." Serena smiled and stood, and then followed the doctor, a tall, slim woman who'd been her doctor on and off for the past couple of years, into the consulting room.

Taking a seat beside the doctor's desk, Serena's stomach churned and her breathing grew faster. She took a deep breath to calm her nerves.

"I have to say, you're looking well, Serena." The doctor peered at her over the rim of her glasses.

"I think it's the hair," Serena replied.

"It could be that. It's certainly different. But anyway, how can I help you today?"

Serena drew another deep breath. "I think I might be pregnant." The words sounded foreign, even though she'd been mulling them over on her tongue for days now. Uttering them out loud to a doctor made them more real.

"Well, let's find out, shall we?"

The doctor took some details and then did an internal examination. As Serena lay on the exam table, she forced herself to breathe slowly. After it was over, the doctor confirmed her suspicions were probably correct. "But I'd like you to have a blood test to be one hundred percent sure."

Serena blew out a breath. "How far along am I?"

"I'd say six to seven weeks, but the blood test will be able to pinpoint more accurately. How do you feel about it, Serena? I'm gathering it wasn't planned."

As she finished redressing, she told the doctor that was correct. It wasn't planned. "I've suspected for a few days now, since I started being sick. Initially I was shocked, but I'm slowly getting used to the idea."

"Does your partner know?"

Serena shook her head. "We're not together at the moment."

"Oh. I see. Do you need some support?"

"I don't think so. My sister-in-law's here with me, and my mother will come if I ask her to. I'll be okay."

"As long as you're sure. The early stages of pregnancy can be a very emotional time and being on your own can compound that."

Yeah, she got that. She smiled at the doctor and thanked her. "I'll get that blood test, and then what?"

"I'll give you a referral to a gynaecologist. I'd probably

suggest that, given what you've been through. You might need a little extra care."

Serena was puzzled. "But surely my burns won't affect the baby."

"No, but you also suffered internal injuries. I think it's wise, that's all. Although you're looking great. The scarring is improving." The doctor's gaze swung to her cheek, and Serena cringed under her scrutiny.

"Maybe," she said, shrugging. "I don't know."

The doctor leaned forward and took both her hands in hers. Her voice was soft with compassion. "Serena, you're doing well. Don't be despondent."

Serena blinked back the sudden tears that stung her eyes. "Thank you. I'm trying not to be."

"I know. You're a strong woman and you'll rise above this." The doctor straightened. "I'm looking forward to seeing you back on television sometime soon. The guy who replaced you simply doesn't cut it."

"If only. I doubt I'll be going back, especially since I'm pregnant now."

"Yes, I understand, but perhaps it's something to work towards."

"Yeah, maybe." She didn't say she already knew that getting her old job wasn't an option. It was irrelevant now. She stood and thanked the doctor again for her time.

"I'll see you again after you've had the test done."

"Okay." Serena smiled again and exited the room.

As she entered the waiting room, Emma looked up expectantly. Serena gave a nod before making her payment at the reception desk and joining her.

Standing, Emma embraced her and held her tight. Serena struggled to contain her tears as she felt genuine love flowing from her sister-in-law. Yes, she would get through this. It wasn't what she'd planned, but somehow, underneath, she sensed that God had it under control.

CHAPTER 21

After they left the medical centre, Serena accepted Emma's offer to spend the day together. They might be sisters-in-law, but they weren't what you would call friends, and normally she would have made some feeble excuse, citing something or other she needed to attend to, thanked her for being there to hold her hand, and then gone her own way. But having received the confirmation that she was indeed pregnant, being with someone who'd been pregnant twice was comforting.

Emma suggested they walk along the waterfront, grab an early lunch, and then perhaps take in a movie. Since Serena had nothing better to do, she agreed.

Strolling along the path that meandered all the way to East Point, they fell into an easy conversation, which was surprising. She'd never spent any time alone with Emma. Jeremy and the children were always around whenever they saw each other, which wasn't that often with Serena spending a lot of time overseas. It was strange at first, and she wasn't sure what they would talk about, but Emma was a chatty person and Serena soon found herself opening up to her.

"I'm not sure what I'm going to do," she said as her gaze locked onto two yachts sailing in the gentle breeze, reminding her of the birds she'd admired that day at Goddard Downs. What would it be like to not have a care in the world?

"You mean, about the pregnancy?" There was an edge to Emma's voice, a tinge of alarm.

Serena turned and faced her. Emma's round eyes had enlarged, and Serena winced. She understood how her statement might have caused concern. "No. I meant about life in general. Not the pregnancy. Sorry."

"Oh. I thought you meant—"

"No, I'm not going to have an abortion."

"Phew. I'm so relieved. For a moment there, I thought that's what you meant."

"No, I wouldn't do that. I'll keep the baby, even though I'm going to be a terrible mother."

"No, you won't! I'm sure you'll be great. It might take a bit of time to get used to motherhood, that's all."

"Thanks for your vote of confidence, but I'm not so sure. Anyway, that's only one thing."

"What else is bothering you?"

Serena exhaled and wiped the sweat off her brow. They were between the pockets of trees that offered reprieve from the sun which was now beating down with intense ferocity. "Let's stop for a drink and I'll tell you."

"Great idea. There's a café up ahead."

After they reached it, they chose a table under the shade of an umbrella on the deck and ordered iced lattes and a chocolate brownie each.

"So, what do you want to talk about?" Emma leaned forward on her crossed arms.

Serena hesitated before replying, now a little unsure that it was a good idea to unburden herself to this woman. But who else was there to talk to who would understand? At least Emma knew her circumstances. She released a big breath. "I'm not sure what to do about David. I called him the other night, but I don't know that I should have."

Emma's brows winged down. "Why's that? Isn't it good that you're talking?"

Serena stared at the glass of water in her hands. "I think he assumes we'll get back together and everything will be fine."

"And you don't want to get back together?"

Serena shrugged. "I don't know. As soon as he finds out about the baby, he'll smother me again, worse than before, and I won't handle it properly."

"Talk to him."

"I already have, but I guess I can try again. I'm waiting to hear back from my boss, Danny." Her gaze lifted from her glass to Emma. "I've asked him to look into the fire that killed David's mother and siblings."

Emma's brows lifted. "I didn't know about that."

"He keeps it quiet. I think he lit it."

"Really? And he's not said that before?"

"No. Either he doesn't know, or he knows and has never told me, but he changed after this happened." Serena lifted her hand to her cheek. "He's always had an urge to fix things. To rescue people. He's put his life at risk so many times, but after I was injured in the explosion, he began treating me like I was totally incapacitated. I can only think he's recalling memories having to do with that fire. He was only four at the time, but he might be carrying a lot of guilt about something and trying to make amends by looking after me above and beyond what was necessary. Consciously or sub-consciously, I'm not sure."

"I had no idea. The poor guy."

"Yeah. I think he's pretty mixed up at the moment."

"But it can be dealt with. He doesn't have to carry guilt forever. There *is* a solution."

"God, you mean?"

Emma nodded as their drinks and brownies arrived. She waited until after the waitress left to reply. "Yes. God's in the business of relieving peoples' burdens."

Serena thought about that as she stirred her latte. Although she'd spent the last ten or more years ignoring God, she did know that was the business He was in. Her overnight experience gave testament to it. "Yes, I know." She drew a long breath. "Last night something strange happened to me. I couldn't sleep, so I grabbed the Bible Frank gave me before I left him and Mum, and I started reading it, more with the thought that it might put me to sleep, but the words spoke to me, and I somehow felt lighter."

Emma nodded. "Scripture does that. God speaks to us through it, and as we open our hearts to Him, He can take our burdens and lighten them. He can do that for David, too."

"I'm not sure that he believes in God."

"That's okay. We can pray and ask God to reveal Himself to him. He has His ways and means." She winked.

"I used to be a Christian." Serena stirred the ice around her latte and then took a sip. It was cool and refreshing and the coffee didn't upset her stomach.

"Yes. Jeremy told me you were quite the advocate when you were younger."

"Yeah." She gazed across the bay. "I was interested in the youth leader, and I jumped in to attract him."

"Did it work?"

"For a time. We broke up when I went to uni. I hadn't really understood what true faith was all about, and I started following whatever cause seemed shiny at the time."

"There's a parable about that."

"I think I remember it… is that the one about the sower?"

"That's the one."

"I think I was like the thorny ground. I accepted Jesus, but then I got distracted by the things of the world and I fell away."

"It's never too late to come back."

Serena sighed heavily. "I don't know. I look at you and Jeremy and Mum and Frank, and you're all such good people. And then I look at my dad, and all I see is a hypocrite. He went to church every Sunday, but he used people during the week. And then there's this." She raised her hand to her cheek again. "If God loves me, why did He let this happen?"

Emma looked at her kindly. "There's no easy answer, but basically, we see the world and what happens to us through our human eyes, not through God's. His plans are so much greater than we can ever imagine. Our vision is so limited, and we tend to place the emphasis on things that don't really matter, but when we get a picture of His immensity and how He sacrificed His Son, despite the fact that He didn't have to, handing us a lifeline so we can live forever with Him, our focus shifts from these less important things to those that really matter, and that will last into eternity."

"Like what?"

"Like loving our neighbours. Caring for the poor. Living life with open hearts and hands. Living like Jesus did. Putting Him first."

"Yeah. Mum's been telling me that kind of thing on and off for years but I ignored it. But now…" She placed her hands on her stomach. "Realising I'll have a baby to care for and raise has made me start thinking about the bigger things."

"A baby is a miracle of God. It's such an amazing time as you watch him or her develop and grow into a little person with their own unique characteristics and personality. Anyone who says God isn't involved in this process hasn't opened their minds, because it's mind blowing." Emma leaned forward, her eyes sparkling. "Did you know that right now, your baby already has a basic nervous system connected to a tiny heart? That soon he or she will have a tailbone and tiny bumps that will become fingers, and that by eight weeks, the brain will start developing? It's amazing and still blows me away whenever I think of it. The process of a developing life is so complex and finely tuned. How anyone could say it isn't a miracle from God is beyond me."

"Wow. You're really passionate about this, aren't you?"

She chuckled. "I guess I am. But all I'm saying is that it's so easy to see things from our human perspective only, but if we do that, we miss out on so much."

Serena leaned back in her chair. "I think I'll do some more reading when I go home, but it doesn't answer my question of what to do about David. Or my job. I got offered the job of host of the talk-back show yesterday, but I don't think I'll take it."

"You'd be great at it."

"You think?"

Emma nodded. "But why don't you pray about it all? You can trust God to guide you."

"Maybe you're right. Maybe I'm worrying too much."

"Seems like it. But that's normal. We all worry. But remembering that God can and does take care of things is a great relief." She smiled. "Would you like me to pray for you now?"

"Here?" Serena glanced around. The café wasn't overly busy. A group of three women sat at a table on the other side of the deck, deep in conversation, and an older man and woman were drinking coffee while gazing across the bay.

"Yes. Why not?"

Serena shrugged. "It feels a little strange, that's all."

"We'll be discreet, okay?"

Serena gave a small chuckle. "Okay." She wasn't quite sure how that would work, but when Emma simply closed her eyes and took a slow breath, Serena did likewise.

"Dear Lord," Emma began in a quiet voice, "please bless Serena and give her confidence that You are with her, that she's not alone through all of this. You knew before time began that she would be carrying this baby, that David would be struggling with guilt, and that Serena would suffer these life-changing injuries. Lord, all of these things seem overwhelming, and yet we know that You provide the strength to face them. Let Serena turn her worries over to You because we know You care for her.

"It's hard sometimes to understand why things happen, but

we don't see the big picture like You do. We place our focus on things that don't matter so much, but You want us to seek first Your Kingdom. Lord, I pray for this little baby that Serena's carrying. An unexpected blessing that will change her life forever. Let her and David work things out that they might be wonderful parents. Lord, we thank You that You are a God who truly cares. One we can turn to in times of trouble, and One we know who listens. Help Serena to come to that place where she can say with confidence that You are her refuge and strength, a very present help in times of trouble. May she experience the peace that comes from a right relationship with You. I pray all these things in Jesus' Name. Amen."

Serena swallowed hard. She wasn't used to praying aloud. She wasn't used to praying, period. But she felt a quickening in her spirit and when she opened her mouth, the words tumbled out. "Lord, I do give all these things to You. I don't understand why they've happened, but I'm prepared to trust You. Help me to do that. Thank You for loving me. Amen." Tears gathered in her eyes, and like they had the night before, her burdens seemed lighter, as if someone else was carrying them for her. She raised her head and smiled at Emma. "Thank you."

Emma squeezed her hand and returned her smile. "You're more than welcome. And you're more than welcome to come to church with us, or to my ladies Bible study group."

Whoa. She hadn't signed up for any of that. She gave a small smile and said she'd think about it.

"That's fine. The door's always open. Now, shall we get an early lunch while we're here?"

"Sounds good. I might even be able to face food today without throwing up."

"That's a good sign. I was sick all the way through to six months with Sebastian. It was such a struggle, but with Chloe, it was much better."

Serena smiled politely. There may have been a shift in her heart, but she still couldn't see herself as a mother, nor could she see herself talking about babies and pregnancy to other people so easily any time in the future. It all seemed so foreign and strange. But her life had taken some strange turns over the past few months, and this was another one. Unless something unforeseen happened, in seven and a half months, she would have a baby, and she would be a mother. The thought made her pulse beat erratically before she reminded herself to simply trust.

CHAPTER 22

All day, David weighed up if he should call Serena that night. Hope that she might take him back, or perhaps even marry him, boosted his spirits, and he was even contemplating returning to Darwin to be with her. He'd be able to get compassionate leave. His mates would understand—they all knew about the horrific injuries Serena had sustained. In fact, they'd probably encourage him to go. Plus, he was concerned about her.

Maybe he should simply go. If he told her he was coming, he ran the risk of her telling him not to. It might be better to surprise her. These thoughts ran around in his head all day as he and the others tried to outsmart yet another fire front that had flared up overnight.

When they arrived back at camp, he pulled Troy aside after dinner and spoke with him. "I'm worried about Serena and I'm thinking about going home."

"Mate, don't worry about us. If you're concerned about her, you should go."

"That's what I thought you'd say. I'm just not sure it's the right thing to do."

"We could be here for another month. Can you wait that long?"

David raked a hand through his hair. "Probably not, but I feel bad about letting you all down."

"You've done your bit, mate. In fact, you've done more than your bit. You don't owe us anything."

David drew a slow breath. "Okay. I'll give it some more thought."

Troy clapped him on the back. "Don't think too hard or you might talk yourself out of it. If she's reached out to you, it might mean she needs help."

"Yeah. I think you're right. She didn't sound good last night."

"Well, pack your bags and get on the first flight out of here."

"As long as you're sure."

"Yeah, mate. Off you go. And I'll be sure to pray for you. Okay?"

"Thanks." David still thought that was a strange thing for Troy to do, but he hadn't forgotten the calmness he'd felt after he'd prayed for him the other night. "I'll speak with the commander and see when I can leave."

"Goodo. And if you want to chat afterwards, you know where I'll be."

David nodded. "Yeah, mate. I might do that."

He left Troy and walked through the camp until he reached the community centre that had been commandeered by the Fire Services as the control building for the region. Although it was after hours, he knew Commander Grierson would still be there. The man barely slept, or when he did, he grabbed only a few hours on the camp stretcher set up beside his desk.

The lights were on as David approached. He walked up the stairs and knocked quietly as he poked his head around the corner. "Excuse me, sir, could I have a word?"

"Sure, come in, son." The man, one of the most respected and experienced fire fighters in the force, waved him in. In his late sixties, he still had a good head of hair, although it was greying, and he wore glasses that he removed as David entered. "Take a seat."

David sat on the opposite side of the desk. "I won't take up much of your time, sir. I'm wanting to take compassionate leave."

The man grunted. "Family problems?"

"Kind of. I'm worried about my partner, Serena."

"She's the one with the burns, isn't she?"

"Yes, that's her." David groaned inwardly. Serena would hate being referred to like that.

"We'll certainly miss you, Kramer, but leave is granted. Thanks for your efforts."

"Thank you, sir. I appreciate it." He stood and started to leave.

"Shut the door behind you."

"Will do." David chuckled as he walked out. No wonder the man was good at his job. No time for chit chat.

David headed back to camp and spoke to the head of the transport section and arranged a lift back to Canberra the following morning. He'd grab a flight from there and would be back in Darwin by mid-afternoon.

As he went to find Troy, his phone rang. Expecting it to be Serena, he answered quickly, without realising the ring tone wasn't hers until it was too late. It wasn't Serena. It was his Aunt Peg telling him that his father had been taken to the hospital and wasn't expected to live. His liver was failing from alcohol abuse, and if David wanted to see him before he passed, he needed to come home.

He told her he was already coming, and that he'd be back the next afternoon.

"That's good, David. I don't think he'll last longer than that."

After the call ended, he slumped against a tree trunk and slipped all the way to the ground and held his head in his hands. He'd not spent much time with his father following the fire that killed his mother and siblings. His father had drunk himself into a stupor and disappeared from his life, only resurfacing every now and then to go into a rehab facility to dry out before starting the cycle all over again. But he was the only one who knew what truly happened that night. If he died, the truth would die with him, and then David might never know and his nightmares would continue forever.

He needed to get home before his father died, but suddenly, the prospect of discovering the truth seemed overwhelming. If he discovered he was responsible for the death of his mother and siblings, how could he live with that degree of guilt? Troy's words came back to him… *I know only one way of dealing with things like this—prayer.* He needed to find Troy. Ask him to pray for him again, because his head felt like it was about to explode.

He found Troy sitting at an outside table chatting with a few of the others. He looked up as David approached. He must have seen the despair on his face because he stood and guided him away from the table. "What's up, mate? Didn't you get leave?"

"Yeah, mate. It's not that. My dad's dying."

"I didn't know he was still alive."

"Yeah, but he's been pretty much dead since the fire. He's an alcoholic." He felt like he was holding raw emotion in check and that any moment, it would tumble out.

"Oh. I'm sorry to hear that."

"It's my fault."

"What do you mean?"

"He started drinking after the fire." He squeezed the sides of his head with his hands. He had to stop the noise. "If I lit it—"

"Stop right there. I know where you're going, and it's not a good place."

"But—"

"No buts. You were a kid. He's an adult. He's responsible for his own behaviour."

"It's easy to say that, but I don't know what to do with this guilt." He couldn't control the spasmodic trembling inside him. Tears spilled from his eyes and rolled down his cheeks.

"I told you before. For a start, you don't know what happened for sure, and even if you did light it, you can't turn the clock back. There's only one cure for guilt, and that is to hand it to God and allow Him to take care of it."

"I don't understand how that works."

"Do you want me to explain it to you?"

"Not now. I need to pack and get ready to leave first thing in the morning."

"That will take you all of five minutes."

David knew that, but he wasn't in any mood for a sermon. "How about you just pray for me?" He wiped his face with his sleeve.

"I can do that. Would you like me to pray now?"

"Okay." He bowed his head as Troy placed his hand on his shoulder, drawing a slow breath to calm his spinning head.

"Lord, I pray once again for my friend, David. His heart is heavy and burdened with guilt. May he lay that guilt at the foot of the cross and be freed from the chains that bind him. May he experience the peace and freedom that comes from a right relationship with You. And Lord, I bring David's father before you. I know nothing about him, but it seems he's lived a troubled life. As that life is possibly coming to an end, may he consider his eternal destiny, and may he seek You, because it's written in Your word that You will never turn away anyone who seeks You with all their heart. I pray all these things in Jesus' precious name. Amen."

"Amen," David whispered. He wasn't sure what had happened when Troy prayed, but something inside him shifted. He couldn't explain it and he didn't understand it, but it seemed God *was* doing something like Troy had asked. It seemed weird. Maybe, like Troy was suggesting, he had a soul, a spiritual side that might live on after the physical body died. If that was true, it was worth exploring. But not now. He needed to pack and get some sleep, although he somehow doubted his mind would allow that to happen. But he had to try. "Thanks," he said, smiling gratefully.

Troy nodded. "You're more than welcome. And I'll keep praying for you. Just remember that you're not alone. God loves you and He wants you to reach out to Him. Okay?"

"Okay. I'll try."

"Do you want to have a drink with the boys before you pack?"

David hesitated. He'd rather simply go and pack and slip away quietly without any fanfare, but they were his buddies and he should at least tell them he was leaving. "Okay. Just a quick one."

"Good man." Troy clapped his shoulder as they strolled back to join the group of six men sitting around the table, chatting and drinking. They all looked bone tired, their smudged faces bearing witness to yet another hard day of work. Troy broke the news to them that David was leaving. As expected, they all said they'd miss him but wished him well. He had one drink and then left to take a shower and prepare for his trip home.

CHAPTER 23

The day seemed endless. After arriving in Canberra at nine a.m., David grabbed a taxi to the airport but had to wait two hours for a flight. And it wasn't a direct one. He had to fly first to Sydney then wait another hour-and-a-half there before boarding a flight to Darwin which would arrive at four o'clock.

He called his auntie several times to check on his father's condition. He was weakening by the hour, and she wasn't sure how long he had. "He has moments of lucidness, and he keeps asking for you."

All David could do was pray that he would get there before his father passed. Once, he tried talking with him on the phone, but he was rambling and David couldn't understand what he was saying.

Troy had given him a book to read. He wasn't a reading man, but he gave it a go. It probably was an all right book, but the words swam on the page. He closed it and slid down in his seat and closed his eyes as he waited for the connecting flight to be called. He didn't realise he'd fallen asleep until someone nudged him. The flight had been called but he hadn't heard it. He gathered his belongings and joined the line.

Settled into his window seat, he gazed over Sydney as the plane lifted and headed north. Soon the ground below became so distant it was hard to see anything. He took the book out again and read the blurb on the back cover. It was called 'Jesus the Bloke', written by a guy named Jason Elsmore.

"I reckon most Aussie blokes would like Jesus if they met Him. They just haven't been introduced to Him very well...yet."

Jesus the Bloke shines a light on Jesus in a uniquely Australian way. Regular Aussie blokes will relate to Jason's stories of growing up in suburban Australia, seeking out adventure wherever possible. Jason shares his own story of faith and the eternal story of Jesus to introduce Aussie blokes to Him in a new way.

Jason's hope is that Aussie blokes who know Jesus will buy this book for a mate who doesn't.

David grunted and turned to the first page. He was surprised that when the hostess came around to serve refreshments, he was on page twenty. The author had an easy-to-read style of writing. It was almost like he was in the seat beside him having a chat, and what he had to say seemed to make sense. David hadn't heard about this Jesus before. The author had written that *He was a good bloke to go fishing with, to have a drink with. To have around when you're hungry. He's a good bloke to know when you're broke. He's a good bloke to have in a boat, and a good bloke to know when you're sick or even when you're dead.* David had chuckled at that and read on. By the time he arrived in Darwin, he'd finished the book and had decided he wanted to know this Jesus for himself. But first, he needed to see his father.

Once out of the terminal, he jumped in a taxi and asked the driver to take him to Darwin Base Hospital. He also called his auntie, his father's older sister, to say he was on his way. He wasn't prepared for her announcement that his father had died ten minutes earlier. It was like the rug had been pulled from under his feet. The wind taken from his sails. A punch to his guts. *How could God have allowed him to die before he got there?*

Tears filled his eyes as the taxi whisked him to the hospital. After paying the driver, he climbed out and headed inside to find his auntie.

She was in the general ward sitting room. It had been a while since he'd seen her. Several years, in fact. They weren't close. After he'd gone to live with his other auntie, his mother's sister, after the fire, he didn't see his father's relatives much, but as an adult, he'd made an effort to get to know them. He wasn't sure why, but guessed it had something to do with wanting to belong.

Auntie Peg was in her mid-sixties, although she always seemed old to him. She was of average height and carried quite a lot of weight. She struggled to stand when he entered the room, and he hurried over to help her. Her eyes were red and she looked distressed. He bent down and hugged her. "I'm so sorry, Auntie."

She sobbed against his chest for a long time. He wondered why she was there on her own. Tom, her second husband had died several years earlier, but she had two adult children, Charlie and Amanda. His cousins. Not that he ever saw them. "You're here on your own?" he asked as he rubbed her back.

She nodded. "Charlie said he'll come soon." She pulled away from him and dabbed her eyes.

"Good," David said. "So, the old blighter couldn't hang on until I got here."

"I know. I kept telling him you were on your way. He was in a terrible state, Davey." Tears spilled from her eyes again. "He was in so much pain."

"Did he say anything?"

"He said he was sorry."

A heavy breath flew from his mouth. Sorry. *Sorry for what? For walking out and leaving him when he was all he had left? For dying before he got there? For not waiting so he could ask what really happened the night of the fire?* He shook his head and walked to the window as more tears threatened to fall. Now he'd never know, and he'd have to carry that burden with him for the rest of his life.

No, you won't. I can take it from you.

David blinked. *Where did that come from?* But he knew. It was the soft voice of Jesus the bloke. *Come to Me, all you who are weary and burdened, and I will give you rest. Take My yoke upon you and learn from Me, for I am gentle and humble in heart, and you will find rest for your souls.*

He wiped his eyes and nodded. *Okay, I will.* After a few moments, he turned and re-joined his auntie.

"Do you want to see him?"

David nodded. "Yes."

"He's down this way." She walked with him through the ward until they reached a curtained off cubicle. The nursing staff hadn't moved his body yet, and it seemed strange that a dead person would be amongst the living. Auntie Peg pulled the curtain aside and asked the nurse if they could go in. She said they could, finished what she was doing, and then left them in private.

Although he should have been prepared for the way his father looked, David wasn't. He'd seen dead people before, but this was different. His father was thin to the point of gauntness, almost a shadow. His skin, grey and withered. David had to fight the urge to lash out at him, even in death. What kind of father would drink himself stupid and leave a four-year-old to fend for himself after just losing his mother? A broken one. That's all he could think of. His father must have loved his mother so much he couldn't bear the thought of living without her. And now he was dead. And the truth of that night had died with him. *Why hadn't he asked him before?* He gave him a hostile glare. Because it was taboo, that's why. His father had never wanted to talk about it. It was like the tragedy had never happened.

David slumped onto the chair beside the bed and stared at him, swallowing hard, trying not to show his anger in front of his aunt.

Her hand rested on his shoulder. "He was a sorry man, Davey. After your mum died, he lost his way. He didn't mean to hurt you."

He shrugged as if her words were of no consequence, but they slid under his bones and tugged at his heart. He couldn't bear the sight of him anymore. "I need to go." Standing, he pushed past her and fled through the ward, sucking in big gulps of air as he reached the outside. Collapsing onto a bench, he struggled to catch his breath as he buried his face in his hands. Hot tears began to fall on the ground, but he didn't care.

Moments passed. Finally, his breathing returned to normal and his tears dried. He wasn't sure why the death of his father, a man he barely knew, had affected him so much, other than it marked the end of the link with his mother and siblings, and that fateful night. He looked up. Auntie Peg stood in front of him with his cousin Charlie beside her. "Are you okay, Davey? I was worried about you."

He nodded. "Yes. It was just the shock of seeing him." That wasn't the complete truth, but she didn't need to hear about his anguish.

"Would you like to come home with us? It's not good for you to be alone."

"I need to see Serena."

"Okay. But you're welcome at any time."

"Thank you. I guess we'll need to make arrangements."

"We can do that tomorrow."

"Okay. I'll call you."

"Great. Can we drop you home?"

"That would be good. Thank you." However, as the words flowed from his mouth, a heavy weight landed in his stomach.

Serena didn't know he was back. *What if she didn't want to see him?*

CHAPTER 24

*D*avid thanked Auntie Peg and Charlie for the ride and then paused outside the apartment block as they drove away, unsure of how Serena would react to his sudden reappearance. Maybe he should call her, at least warn her he was on his way up. But what if she told him to go away like she had the last time he'd seen her? But then he remembered that she'd told him she loved him the other night on the phone. No, he'd just go up. He wouldn't call.

His heart pounded as he entered the building, and dreams of holding her again filled his heart and mind. A dizzying current raced through his body, fuelled by the emotion of his father's death and anticipation of being with Serena. Their time apart seemed like an eon. He felt breathless as he sprinted up the stairs, not bothering to wait for the lift.

Placing his key into the door, he paused. There was no noise. No music. No television. Perhaps she was asleep. His shoulders fell. *Perhaps she wasn't there.* He turned the key and opened the door, quickly realising the apartment was empty. She wasn't home.

He swallowed the disappointment creeping up his throat and walked inside, dumping his bag on the tiled floor of the entry. The apartment was a lot tidier and cleaner than when he'd left that day in a hurry. In fact, at a quick glance, it looked like she'd done a spring clean.

After grabbing a drink of water, weariness enveloped him and he fell onto the couch, but sleep didn't come. He needed to see her. He couldn't wait for her to come back from wherever she was. Sitting, he pulled out his phone and called her. She answered after three rings. "David." Her voice was like balm to his soul.

"Serena, where are you?"

"At Emma and Jeremy's. Why?"

"Can I come over?"

"Are you back?" The surprise in her voice cut through him. She didn't sound overly pleased to hear from him.

"Yes. My father just died." That wasn't the initial reason for his return, but she didn't need to know that. Not yet, anyway.

"Oh. I'm sorry."

"It's okay." He raked his hand across his hair.

"I…I guess it's all right for you to come over."

"Good. I'll leave now. I should be there within half an hour."

"Okay. See you then."

He ended the call and decided to grab a quick shower before heading out, but as he entered the bathroom, her smell filled his nostrils and desire for her overwhelmed him. He loved her. That was all there was to it. He held her towel to his face and breathed in her scent as he imagined crushing her to him and kissing her passionately. But then he came back to earth with a thud. He needed to tread carefully. Something about her tone was different. He would need to woo her. Not assume she was his.

He stepped into the shower and scrubbed himself head to foot. The full-sized shower with no time restriction was a luxury, but he couldn't stay and enjoy it.

After drying himself, he dressed quickly and headed out. She'd probably taken the car, but he checked the garage in case she hadn't. He was surprised to see it there, so he unlocked it, climbed in, and was soon on his way to her brother's place.

Pulling up outside the four-bedroom house in the suburbs, his heart pounded. This time, he knew she was inside. He stepped out and walked quickly up the driveway. Jeremy and Emma's white Prado was parked in the carport, and beyond it under the shade of a large white cloud tree was a trampoline with safety mesh around the sides and a bike with training wheels lying on its side. The front porch was tiny and just two steps up. He took them as one, and standing poised at the door, swallowed hard.

As he lifted his hand to knock, Emma appeared at the door, baby Chloe in her arms, her face as jolly and bright as always. "David, come in!" She opened the door and gave him a warm, one-armed hug.

He hugged her back, smiled, said hello, and stepped inside while peering around, looking for Serena.

"She's having a rest. Sorry."

"Oh." Disappointment weighed him down again. Why would she be resting when she knew he was coming?

"Jeremy's out the back. Would you like to go through?"

"Sure. Thanks." He shoved his hands into his pockets and sauntered through the house. Toys and books were strewn over the floor of the family room, and the kitchen counter was covered with unwashed cooking utensils. The aroma of curry hung in the air, and his stomach rumbled. Maybe he could make good on that rain check and stay for dinner.

Jeremy was kicking a ball around with Sebastian, but he stopped and hurried over and shook David's hand. "Good to see you, Dave. Sorry to hear about your dad."

David shrugged and gave a nod. "Thanks. We weren't that close, but it was still a shock. How's your dad doing, by the way?"

Jeremy's countenance changed before his eyes, his shoulders drooping and a flash of sadness crossing his face. "Not great at all. Looks like he's got a psychotic disorder, possibly bipolar. It's too early to tell, but he's not doing very well."

"I'm sorry to hear that. Seems like both our dads are causing us grief at the moment."

"Yeah. Seems that way. Can I get you a drink?"

"What are you offering?"

"Coke. Juice. Water."

He'd love a beer, but Jeremy didn't drink alcohol, so it was no use asking. "Coke would be fine, thanks."

Jeremy poked his head inside and asked Emma for two Cokes.

"Can I have one, too, Daddy?" Sebastian tugged on his shirt

and asked in such a sweet voice that David had no idea how Jeremy could deny the request, but he did. "No, mate. Coke's for grown-ups. You can have water."

Sebastian's lip protruded in a pout until Jeremy gave him a stern look. The pout quickly disappeared and he ran off to kick the ball. David chuckled. He'd never really thought about having kids, but seeing the way Jeremy and Sebastian interacted and looked so comfortable with each other made him wonder what it would be like to have a child. He couldn't imagine Serena ever wanting them, so it probably would never happen. But he was getting ahead of himself. They weren't back together again yet.

As he accepted the icy cold can from Jeremy, he glanced at the back windows of the house. Was she in one of the rooms? Had she heard him arrive? Had she peeked through the blinds and snatched a glimpse of him? His heart beat faster. Any minute now he might see her. But it would be awkward, in front of Jeremy and Emma. After all, they'd barely spoken since she turned down his proposal and he'd stormed off after she'd said some horrid words to him. He still cringed every time he thought of them. She'd only said them in the heat of the moment. She didn't really mean them, but words held power, and once spoken were hard to retract, leaving memories that held a bitter taste. But he'd push it aside, if only she'd take him back.

Jeremy held up his can. "Cheers, mate. Good to have you back."

"Thanks," David replied as they clinked cans and sat around an oblong, glass-topped table. "So, how's Serena doing?"

If David wasn't mistaken, Jeremy blinked several times before he replied, "Good." He said it a little too glibly, as if trying to sound convincing, and it gave David cause for concern. His forehead creased. It was unusual for her to be visiting Jeremy and Emma. He'd never known her to be close to them, even though Jeremy was her only sibling. And for her to be taking a nap in one of their bedrooms? Something was wrong.

"Are you sure?"

Jeremy nodded. "She's tired, that's all. It could be her new hair colour. Who knows? She's dyed it pink. Did she tell you?"

"No, she didn't. Pink?"

He chuckled. "Yes. And it doesn't look too bad."

"Right. Well, I guess I'll see it soon."

"Yes. I expect she's heard you."

∼

MIXED FEELINGS SURGED through Serena as she perched on the edge of the single bed in Jeremy and Emma's guest room. Knowing David was outside waiting to see her had caused a knot in her stomach and a lump in her throat. His deep, familiar masculine voice drifting in through the window reached inside and tugged at her heart. Part of her wanted to race outside and throw her arms around him and tell him she loved him. Tell him about the baby. Say she was sorry. But the other part knew that if she did, there would be no turning back.

Conflicted, she stood and paced the room, but she couldn't

hide in there forever. She had to go outside and face him. *God, what should I do?* Her breaths came fast. Why was it so hard? She loved David, and she knew he loved her.

Trust Me...

She stopped pacing. Yes. That's what she needed to do. Trust. They were adults. They could work this out. Taking a deep breath, she opened the door and stepped out of the room.

∼

DAVID'S HEART skipped a beat when Serena emerged through the doorway. His gaze immediately landed on her pink hair but then swept over her from head to foot. He barely noticed her scarred cheek, and even if he had, it didn't worry him. He went to her and embraced her gently, although every fibre in his being wanted to hold her tight, kiss her passionately, say he loved her, but her mere touch soothed his soul. "You're looking good, babe." He kissed her hair, breathed in her scent, and then released her.

"I'm sorry about your dad," she said.

Transfixed, he gave a half-smile while gazing into her eyes. "Thanks. I got there ten minutes after he passed."

"Oh. That's sad."

He nodded. She had no idea how sad it was. He swallowed hard. He had to address his guilt at some time, but right now, he only had eyes for her.

Jeremy cleared his throat. "We'll take a walk and leave you two to chat."

David blinked. For a moment he'd forgotten they weren't alone. "Are you sure?"

"Yes. We'll go to the park and be back for dinner."

"Thank you." David faced him and nodded, then returned his attention to Serena. "Do you want a drink?"

She shook her head.

"Sit with me?" He headed to the table and hoped she'd follow. She did. She chose a chair opposite him.

Silence filled the air. There was so much he wanted to say to her, but he didn't know where to start. He tried to hold her gaze, read her mind, see her heart, but she tore her gaze away and stared at her hands.

"Serena," he finally said. "I'm not sure where we stand, but I want to start again with you. Without you in my life, it means nothing."

Her gaze didn't shift, but he saw her swallow. Perhaps even blink back a tear. She was tormented, and he wanted to comfort her, but he daren't lest he lose her.

"Things changed between us after I went to you in Paris, and I'm sorry I smothered you. I wasn't fully aware of it until you told me when I proposed that night. When I saw your injuries, something came over me and I had this desperate need to look after you. I now think I know what triggered it." He waited, hoping, praying she would look at him.

Seconds passed. His heart pounded. If he lost her now…

And then she lifted her head and found his gaze. "Tell me what happened, David." Her voice was soft. Calm. Measured.

He swallowed hard. Drew a deep breath. "I think my subconscious told me that if I looked after you really well, in some way I'd be atoning for my mother's death. Rationally, that doesn't make any sense, but I've been having dreams. Nightmares, really." He swallowed hard again. "I think I lit the fire." His throat grew thick as he uttered the words.

She held his gaze. "I've thought that too."

"I wanted to know for sure, but only my father knew the truth, and now he's dead." His voice caught and tears welled in his eyes.

She moved around the table and cradled his head in her arms as tears spilled down his cheeks and deep, guttural sobs rose from a place in his soul he wasn't aware existed until recently. "It's okay, hon. Even if you lit it, I'm sure you didn't mean to kill your mother. You were probably only playing with matches."

He nodded as he wiped his tears. She was probably right, but pain still squeezed his heart.

"Maybe you'll never know, but you can't change what happened, and you can't bring her back. The only thing you can do is let go of your guilt and live your life in a way that would make her proud of you."

He nodded again. "That's what Troy told me."

"Troy?"

"He's a mate and we chatted a bit while we were down south. He helped me when I was having nightmares."

"I'm glad you had someone."

He sniffed. "Yes." He placed his hand over hers and squeezed gently, her warmth enveloping him like a soft blanket. "Are we going to be alright, Serena?" He tilted his head, hoping, praying she would say yes.

Moments passed. His pulse raced. How could he live if she said no?

"I'm…I'm not sure, David. So much has happened…"

"But we can figure it out."

"Maybe."

Standing and facing her, he lifted his hand to her good cheek and gazed into her eyes. "I know we can. I'll do better, Serena. I love you." His whisper held a thread of pain.

Her eyes misted over. "I don't know, David. I need time. So much has changed."

"Like what, babe?"

She shrugged and looked like she was about to burst into tears. "I can't talk about it."

He was confused. What could possibly have changed so much? "Come on, babe. Whatever it is, I'm here for you."

She inhaled deeply and for a moment her eyes darted everywhere until they settled on his. "Okay… I'm…I'm pregnant."

His eyes felt like they could pop out of his head. "You're pregnant?"

She nodded.

"That's great news, isn't it?"

She released her breath. "I'm not used to the idea yet. I only found out for sure today."

"But you're okay with it?"

She rubbed her neck. "Not really. Having kids never featured in my plans, but I will get used to it. Maybe it's the change I need."

"I'll be there for you all the way, babe."

"That's the problem, David. If things are going to work between us, we need to start at the beginning. I can't go back to how it was. Plus, you're going to think this strange, but I've been reconnecting with my faith, and I'm not sure how that will work with us."

"Really? That *is* strange, because Troy's been talking to me about God. In fact, he gave me a book to read on the plane."

"No way. I don't believe it."

He nodded. "It's true. He started talking to me when I was having my nightmares. He told me God could help with my guilt."

"I think He can. I wasn't going to tell you this, but I asked Danny to look into the fire."

"You did?"

She nodded. "I guessed you were blaming yourself and I wanted to know if there was any proof."

"And?"

"I haven't heard back from him yet."

"I looked it up on the internet but there was nothing conclusive. That's why I wanted to ask my dad."

"We have access to a lot of information, so you never know, Danny might find something."

Maybe he would find out the truth after all. And maybe, finally, the shadows of the past could be dealt with. "That would be amazing. Thank you. But what are we going to do? I'll do whatever you want, babe, as long as we can be together."

"I'm not sure, but if Emma and Jeremy are agreeable, I'll stay here for a while, and we can date."

His forehead furrowed. *"Date?"*

She nodded. "What's wrong with that?"

"Nothing. It just seems an odd thing to do after living together for six years."

"But we haven't, not really. It was an on and off again relationship, and to make it work, we have to do it properly. Treat it seriously. I'm prepared to work at it for the baby's sake. Are you?" Quirking a brow, she threw the challenge at him.

What choice did he have? He loved her, and he wanted her in his life forever, so he had to agree. It wasn't ideal, but without hesitation, he said, "Of course I will."

"Good. I know it'll be hard, but I really believe it's for the best. We can still spend lots of time together, but we need to work through things." She paused, and a grin spread across her face. "And besides, it might be fun. We can do things people do when they're dating, like go to the movies, take walks, eat out."

His mind worked overtime. She must have turned a corner, because prior to going to Brampton Downs for her mother's wedding, she'd barely ventured outside. "I'd love to do those things with you, babe."

"Good. And perhaps we can fit in a trip to see Mum and Frank. I haven't told her about the baby yet."

"I'm sure we can do that. I don't have much leave left, but I can take some more time off without pay."

She smiled. "That would be great. It's lovely out there, and I think you'll enjoy it. We could even go on an overnight cattle drive. They asked me to go on one before I came back, but I wasn't in the right frame of mind then, but things have changed." As she held his gaze and he looked deep into her eyes, his heart raced as he sensed a longing in her to be kissed. He nudged her chin up with his thumb and then traced her jaw line with his finger. "Serena, I love you with my whole being, and I'll do whatever it takes to convince you. I'm sorry for what happened in the past, but let's begin again and do it right this time."

She nodded and lifted her mouth to his. Waves of warmth rippled through his body; the air in his lungs thinned. Her shallow breaths filled him with a deep longing, rendering him powerless. Cupping her cheeks with his hands, he bent towards her, closing his eyes as his lips brushed hers. A soft groan escaped him as he tasted the lips he'd feared would never be his again. As his kiss deepened, her body melded to his, and she kissed him back with an intensity rivalling his own. Although desire licked through him, to win her back he had to treat her right, so he broke the kiss and searched her eyes. "We need to take it slow, babe. That's what you said, isn't it?"

Nodding, she slipped her arms around his waist and pressed her head to his chest. "Thank you," she whispered.

He held her close and thanked God for bringing her back to him.

Jeremy and Emma returned moments later, their gazes inquisitive but hopeful. "Hey there," Emma said brightly. "Looks like you two are getting on."

The couple shared a smile before he replied, "Yes, you could say that."

"Well, I'm pleased for you. I guess you won't need much convincing to stay for dinner?"

"No, the curry smells amazing."

"Just as well I cooked double." Emma chuckled.

Pulling away from him, Serena offered her help, which Emma gratefully accepted by handing her the baby. "Can you sit with her while I dish up? I'll grab her bottle."

Serena's eyes widened, and she looked a little awkward as she took the little girl from Emma, but it warmed David's heart to see her trying. He had no doubt she'd be a great mother, and by golly, he would be the world's best father.

By the time he left later that evening, he was filled with hope and the promise of wonderful things to come. Serena walked him to the car and they shared another kiss under a starry-filled sky before he reluctantly left her and drove home on his own.

CHAPTER 25

Maggie was busy in the vegetable patch when her phone rang. Quickly removing her gloves, she pulled her phone from her pocket and answered, already knowing it was Serena from the ring tone. "Hey sweetheart. How are you doing?"

"Good. I've got some news for you."

Maggie chuckled. Serena was never one for small talk, but then her heart went into freefall as all the possibilities of what the news could be flashed through her mind. "Oh?" she replied, trying to rein those thoughts in.

"Yes. David and I are back together again."

For a moment, Maggie was speechless, but it was wonderful news, and she said so. "I'm so pleased, sweetheart. I didn't know he was back."

"He came back yesterday. His father died."

"Oh, I'm sorry to hear that. How is he coping?"

"He's doing okay. A lot of things have happened, Mum, and

we were wondering if we could come for a visit after the funeral."

"Of course you can. You're always welcome, you know that."

"Thank you. He's not sure when it will be yet, but I'll let you know."

"We're not going anywhere."

"I figured that. I mentioned to him that we could maybe go on one of those overnight cattle drives. Do you think that would be okay?"

Maggie smiled, her heart warming with gladness at this unexpected turn of events. "I'm sure that can be arranged." Her brows drew together as she thought she heard a baby crying. "Where are you? I thought I heard a baby."

Serena chuckled. "You did. I'm staying at Jeremy and Emma's for a while. David and I are taking our reconciliation slowly, and we've agreed not to live together while we're dating."

"Really? Wow, I have to admit that surprises me, but I think it's wonderful. Your relationship will be the stronger for it."

"I hope so. Anyway, I have to go. I just wanted to tell you."

"Thank you. You've made my day, sweetheart."

When Maggie ended the call, she gave thanks to God for the wonderful news, and as she returned to pulling weeds, she prayed for Serena and David, that their relationship would grow strong, but more than anything, that they would come to know the saving grace of Jesus in their lives and the peace that it brought.

Later, when Frank returned from work and they were having a drink on the deck as the sun slowly went down across the lagoon and the sky changed from blue to a splattering of oranges and pinks, she told him the news. "I couldn't believe it to start with, but I'm so pleased they're working things out. David's a good guy, and Serena sounded happy. It'll be nice to have them both here for a while."

"It will. I'm looking forward to getting to know them."

"Perhaps we could go on a cattle drive with them. Serena said they wanted to go on one while they were here."

"That could be arranged, my love."

"Wonderful. So long as we can have a double swag."

"I think we can arrange that, too." Reaching out, he laced his fingers with hers, bringing her hand to his lips and gently kissing it. His gaze lingered on hers, and a smile that made her insides turn to flame simmered on his lips.

If only David and Serena could experience such wonderful love.

DAYS PASSED, and when Maggie next heard from Serena, she was delighted to hear that she and David were planning on arriving in two days' time. The roads were still closed because the rivers were still flooded, so they would fly to Kununurra and hoped they could get a helicopter ride to Goddard Downs.

"That will be fine, sweetheart. And guess what? You'll be here for our shindig with the neighbours!"

"Oh." A pause. "Maybe we should delay our visit."

"No! Don't do that. It'll be fun. I didn't realise you were planning on coming so soon."

"David said he'd like to get out of town for a bit now that

the funeral's over. He's had some things on his mind and thinks being out in the country will do him good."

"I'm sure it will. Being out here helps clear the mind. And if you'd rather not come to the shindig, I'm sure we can find somewhere else for you to be."

"I'm sure it will be okay. And you might be happy to know that I've started going out without my scarf."

Tears welled in Maggie's eyes. "That's wonderful, Serena. I'm so glad. You've got absolutely nothing to be embarrassed about."

"I know. I'm slowly getting used to it, although I don't know if I'll ever like it."

"Time's a great healer, sweetheart."

"Yes, I know that."

"I'll let Frank know you're coming and that you'll need a helicopter ride. And we'll also book that cattle drive. The rains are easing, so it should be fine, and the boys are keen to do a trial run before the tourist season starts."

"Sounds good. I'll look forward to seeing you soon."

"Likewise, sweetheart." After ending the call, Maggie leaned back in her chair and smiled, elated by the possibilities that lay ahead. Frank had left only moments before but had promised to be back by lunch so they could start preparing for the shindig. She'd only just started reading her daily devotional when Serena rang, so she opened the book and reread the verses from Psalm 100 which she uttered as her own prayer of thanksgiving.

Shout for joy to the Lord, all the earth.
Worship the Lord with gladness;

> *come before Him with joyful songs.*
> *Know that the Lord is God.*
> *It is He who made us, and we are His;*
> *we are His people, the sheep of his pasture.*
> *Enter His gates with thanksgiving*
> *and His courts with praise;*
> *give thanks to Him and praise His name.*
> *For the Lord is good and His love endures forever;*
> *His faithfulness continues through all generations.*

She bowed her head. "Yes, Lord, I give You thanks and praise for Your enduring love and faithfulness that continues through all generations. That's the prayer of my heart, Lord, that Serena and David will come to know You for themselves. Please let their stay here be a real blessing and a time of healing. I pray these things in Jesus' precious name. Amen."

After tidying the breakfast dishes away, she headed outside and climbed onto the bicycle Frank had retrieved from one of the workshops. She liked walking, but riding was quicker, and she needed to get things ready for David and Serena's visit. Her mind had already begun to whirl. They couldn't stay with her and Frank because there was only one bedroom in the cabin. Perhaps Serena could stay in the guest room in the main house and David in one of the eco tents. He'd probably like that, especially if he was needing time to think. Over the past few weeks, she, Olivia and Janella had finished furnishing the tents and they were ready for use. They'd turned out wonderfully well and would be more than comfortable, even for an extended stay, which she hoped it might be.

As she rode along the path, her heart was light and anticipation filled her. After the months of struggle following the blast, when Maggie feared she might never learn to live with her injuries, Serena was finally sounding like herself. But there was something different about her she couldn't quite put her finger on. But it didn't matter; she'd be here in two days!

Reaching the homestead, she parked the bike and ran up the stairs, but the house was empty. Normally there was some noise or smell of baking, but there was nothing and she immediately grew concerned. Where could they all be? She headed to the kitchen. The table hadn't been cleared from breakfast, which she thought strange. Plates with untouched toast and muffins were still in the middle, and mugs of warm tea were on the table. They'd obviously left in a hurry. With a chill running down her spine, Maggie pulled her phone out and called Olivia.

Relief filled her when Olivia answered. "Maggie! Come down to the stables. Pepper's foaling!"

She held her hand to her chest. "Oh. You had me worried when nobody was here."

"Sorry, we should have told you."

"There was no need for me to know. But I'll come down now."

"Good. If you hurry, you should make it in time. Oh, Dad's here. He's doing the delivery."

"Really?"

"Yes. He's the expert with these things."

As Maggie headed out, she recalled that on her first visit to Goddard Downs, Frank had been held up because he was attending to a new calf who was having trouble feeding. It seemed he had a special way with the animals, and that warmed her heart.

She could only imagine how excited the children were, especially Sasha, who was to be given the new foal for her birthday. As she hurried to the stables, she forgot for a moment about Serena and David's visit, but when she finally remembered, she thanked God once again for new beginnings which were all around.

CHAPTER 26

David and Serena's plane arrived on time in Kununurra, and Maggie stood with Frank, her arm linked through his, as she eagerly waited for them to enter the terminal. She'd already seen Serena's pink hair as she and David walked across the tarmac from the plane. It stood out like a pink flamingo. How could she miss it? But she didn't care. It probably suited her, but it didn't matter either way. If it helped her feel better about herself, that was all that mattered.

Within moments, the couple walked through the doors and Maggie rushed towards them, holding her arms out. She hugged Serena first, and then David. "It's great to see you both! I love your hair, Serena."

"You don't have to say that, Mum."

Maggie smiled. "I think it's lovely. It's not my colour, but it suits you."

Serena laughed. "You never know—you could try it."

"I don't think so. But anyway, how was your flight?" Maggie

slipped her arm around Serena's waist as they walked to the luggage carousel.

"Just a flight. Flying makes me queasy these days."

"Oh? That's unusual for you."

Serena shrugged. "Yeah. It's a bit strange."

"I hope you'll be okay in the helicopter."

"I'll be fine."

Maggie smiled. A short while later, as they strolled over to the helicopter, she studied Serena more closely. There was something other than her hair that was different. What was it?

She let David sit in the front with Frank while she joined Serena in the back. "Are you okay, sweetheart?" she mouthed as they took off.

Serena nodded and mouthed back, "Yes, I'm good," but moments later she grabbed the airsick bag from the side pocket and threw up.

Maggie rubbed her back and grabbed a bottle of water from her bag and handed it to her once she settled. "Are you sure you're okay? You're not ill?"

Serena shook her head. "Not ill. Pregnant."

Maggie's eyes widened. "Pregnant!"

Serena nodded as she wiped her mouth.

Maggie was speechless. It was the last thing she'd expected, but once she processed the news, she shifted closer and gave her a hug. "Congratulations, sweetheart." Although she doubted the pregnancy was planned, it was still a blessing, and perhaps the reason why she and David were back together.

"Thank you."

"How are you?"

Serena shrugged again. "Okay."

It wasn't easy to talk with the engine noise and the whir of the rotors, so Maggie took her hand and patted it before turning her gaze to the scenery below. Not that she was really looking at it. How could she after hearing this most unexpected but exciting news?

They landed at Goddard Downs half an hour later. When the engine was cut and the noise subsided, she turned to Serena and asked if it was okay to tell Frank.

"Yes. He may as well know. We were going to tell you together, but then I threw up."

"It's kind of a giveaway, isn't it?"

"Yeah. I wish it would stop."

"It will. Give it time." Maggie squeezed her hand again.

"That's what everybody says," Serena replied as she shuffled across the seat to the door.

"It's true," Maggie said, following her.

When they were on the ground, she faced David and grinned. "I believe congratulations are in order."

His eyes enlarged and his gaze swung to Serena.

She shrugged. "Mum knows. I threw up in the back."

"Oh."

Stretching up, Maggie smiled and placed a kiss on his cheek. "It's great news. Congratulations."

He returned her smile and thanked her.

Frank's brows came together as he joined the group. "Am I missing something?" His gaze shifted between all three.

Maggie sidled up to him and slipped her arm around his waist. "Yes. Serena and David are expecting."

"Wow. That's a surprise." He gave Serena a kiss on the cheek and shook David's hand. "Congratulations."

"Thank you," they replied in unison.

Maggie didn't miss the look of adoration David gave Serena. She wasn't sure what problems he was still dealing with, but one thing she did know, he loved Serena with all his heart, and that made her glad.

Frank ushered them into his truck and drove to the cabin. Maggie had pre-prepared a light lunch—zucchini and bacon quiche, a green salad and crusty bread, which she served on the verandah. Frank was a great conversationalist and quickly put both Serena and David at ease, but Maggie was surprised when David began talking about his father while they were having coffee. She was even more surprised when he talked about the nightmares he'd been having.

Serena reached out and held his hand. "That was one of the reasons we thought coming here would be a good idea. I told him how peaceful it was and that it might help."

Frank nodded. "It's a good place to come when you need to figure stuff out. You can ride out with us one day if you like. Round up some cattle."

David smiled. "I'd like that."

"And what about the overnight cattle drive? Are we able to do that?" Serena asked eagerly.

"Are you sure you're up to it, sweetheart?" Maggie asked without thinking. She winced at the withering look Serena gave her. Some things didn't change. "Sorry. You're not sick, just pregnant. Got it."

Serena gave a nod.

"Yes, the boys checked the weather and tomorrow looks good," Frank replied.

"So soon?" Serena's brows lifted.

"Is that a problem?" Maggie asked.

"No. I just wasn't expecting it to be tomorrow, that's all."

"We'll leave late morning, head south towards Brown's Ridge, camp out overnight near the river, and then head back," Frank explained.

"Sounds good." David stretched his legs and put his hands behind his head. "I haven't been on a horse in a long time, but I'm looking forward to it."

"And what about this shindig?" Serena asked. "When's that?"

"Two days later, on Saturday," Maggie replied.

Serena leaned forward in her seat and rested her crossed arms on the table. "There's one more thing."

Maggie stiffened. She'd had enough surprises for one day, but then she thought that perhaps David had proposed again and this time Serena had accepted. That would make sense. Her body relaxed while she waited for the announcement.

Serena glanced at David and slipped her hand onto his thigh. He gave a nod and straightened.

Maggie waited with bated breath and could barely keep the grin off her face. "Yes. We're waiting," she said.

Serena drew a deep breath. "This will probably come as a surprise, but we've started going to church."

Maggie's jaw dropped. That was not what she was expecting, but it was the best news ever. Even better than an engagement. "Wow, sweetheart. You could have knocked me over with a feather! That's wonderful news. How did it happen?"

Serena explained how she'd started reading the Bible Frank had given her, and how David had read the book Troy had given him. "It just seemed to make sense, that's all. We've both been struggling with different issues, and we've accepted that it's easier to let God fix them than for us to battle them on our own. Jeremy and Emma have been great and have been helping us understand the basics. We have a lot to learn, but we've both made a commitment to follow Jesus and we're excited about what the future holds. Especially with this little bundle on the way." She placed her hands over her stomach and smiled. "Like I said on the phone, a lot has changed."

"It certainly has," Maggie said through tears of joy. God had answered her prayers beyond her wildest dreams and deep gratitude welled inside her as she hugged her daughter.

A short while later, Frank drove them to the homestead where they chatted briefly with Olivia and Janella before dropping Serena's bags in the guest room. They then headed out to the eco tent set up to settle David in.

Since it was only a five-minute easy stroll from the homestead, they opted to walk instead of drive. David had only brought a backpack which he slung over his shoulder.

The tents, six in total, were positioned for privacy amongst the paperbarks and palms and offered either a mountain or lagoon view.

"We figured you'd prefer a mountain view, so we put you in this one, but if you'd rather have a different one, it's not a problem," Maggie said.

"This is perfect." David smiled gratefully as he climbed the three steps, stopping on the deck furnished with a small table and two chairs, a hammock and a gas barbecue, and leaned on the railing while he gazed out. "It's a great view. I think I'll enjoy sitting out here."

"Yes, it's very peaceful," Maggie said. "Now, come inside

and I'll show you around. Not that there's much to show." She laughed. "It's quite compact."

Frank waited outside while Maggie showed David and Serena the inside. She and the girls were proud of the way the tents had come together. This one had a double bed with a light voile canopy. Some of the other tents had two singles. There was also a small bookshelf with games, including a chess set, and a kitchenette with a set of plates, utensils and basic cookware. The lights and fridge were solar powered, and the tent was fully screened, allowing good airflow. There was a shared bathroom facility behind the tents.

"This is lovely. Thank you, Maggie." David smiled as he gazed around. "I'll be very comfortable here."

"You're welcome. You're also welcome to join the family or Frank and me for meals, or you can take them here, whatever you wish. You'll find basic supplies in the cupboard and fridge, and they can be topped up whenever you need."

"Great. You've thought of everything."

"Thank you. We're hoping these tents will be popular during the tourist season."

"I'm sure they will be."

"Now, what would you like to do? Have some time on your own, take a walk or drive, or visit with us?"

His gaze turned to Serena. "Shall we take a walk?"

She nodded. "That would be nice."

"There don't seem to be any storms on the way, so you should be fine. Would you like to have dinner with the family tonight?" Maggie asked.

"Sure. That sounds great. Thank you," Serena replied.

Maggie smiled. "You're welcome."

She left the couple and joined Frank who was strolling through the tropical garden she and the girls had planted. Slipping her hand into his, she smiled. "It's been a day of surprises, hasn't it?"

"It sure has. God is good."

"Yes. I feel so blessed. I still can't believe all this has happened, but it's wonderful."

He turned and faced her, rubbing her forearms with his hands. "You know God works in mysterious ways. We can never pre-empt Him."

"Yes, and yet, so often I do. I tell Him what I want rather than waiting for Him to do what He wants."

Frank chuckled. "I think we're all guilty of that at times."

"You're probably right."

"Now, my beautiful wife, what are we going to do with our afternoon?" He lifted a brow and she knew what he had on his mind, but Maggie had something else she wanted to do.

"Can we take the horses out? I think I need a practice ride before tomorrow."

He chuckled. "Of course we can, although I'm sure you'll be fine."

"It's been a long time since I've ridden."

"But it's something you never forget."

"I hope you're right!"

"Come on then, let's go." He took her hand and they strolled back to the stables to pick up the gear they'd need. The horses were in the top paddock, so they put the gear in the truck and drove. It took Frank twenty minutes to saddle up the horses with Maggie standing by, handing him the gear. He'd chosen an older mare for her called Bella. His horse, Midnight, stood at least two hands higher. He helped her up and then mounted Midnight.

She smiled at him as they headed off and wondered why they hadn't been out riding since they returned from their honeymoon. It was a lovely afternoon, hot, but not unbearably so, and it was wonderful to be out in the fresh air in the midst of this beautiful country. "Where shall we go?" she asked.

"To the lookout?"

"Sounds wonderful. Lead the way!"

They spent a lovely afternoon together, and by the time they returned, Maggie felt more confident about going on the cattle drive the following day. She also suggested they go for a ride together at least a few times a week, and Frank agreed.

CHAPTER 27

After a leisurely afternoon stroll with David, followed by dinner with her mum and Frank, Serena slept soundly in the guest room at Goddard Downs. Although it had only been a few weeks since she'd been there, this time it was different. She had more direction and felt settled, despite her unexpected pregnancy, or perhaps because of it. Knowing she was carrying new life had given her a different perspective, and although she still thought she'd be a terrible mother, the idea of having a child was growing on her. And she had no doubt that David would be a wonderful father. He was trying so hard not to smother her, to give her room to be herself, and she was starting to think that if he proposed again, this time, she'd accept. But it was too soon for that. They still needed time to grow into this new relationship, with each other and with God, before they committed to spending their life together as husband and wife.

Plus, the issue of the fire still remained. David was as

convinced as ever that he'd lit it and was still struggling with guilt, although he'd prayed about it and had been prayed for by Jeremy and Emma. Serena hoped that Danny would find some information soon, one way or the other, although she dreaded having David's fears confirmed. But at least knowing the truth might set him free.

As she awoke to the sun streaming in through the curtains, she wondered how David had slept in the tent. It looked so cosy, and she would have loved to have stayed there with him, but they'd agreed to sleep apart. She had, however, promised to have breakfast with him, not that she would be eating anything other than a piece of dry toast. But as she sat up in bed and for the first time in a long time a wave of nausea didn't greet her, she thought that maybe her sickness had gone. How wonderful that would be!

Climbing out of bed, she slipped on a pair of black denim shorts, a sleeveless white T-shirt and a button up overshirt that she left unbuttoned. Her hair took no time at all these days, although it had finally started to grow a little, but doing her face always took longer. Her scars had become less noticeable, or perhaps she'd simply become less conscious of them. Either way, she wasn't so concerned about how she looked anymore. Her mum had been right—knowing she was loved regardless of how she looked made so much difference as to how she felt about herself.

After making her bed, she slipped on her shoes and opened the door, only to be greeted by the aroma of bacon and eggs wafting down the hallway from the kitchen. For a moment she thought she'd have to make a dash for the bathroom, but the expected nausea didn't come, and she smiled with relief. She'd already told Janella and Olivia she'd be having breakfast with David, so she left by the front door. Not that she didn't want to spend time with them, but there'd be plenty of time for socialising later.

It was a gorgeous day, and while strolling along the gravel path, inhaling the fresh, clean air and listening to the birds tweeting and chirping, her heart lifted and she had a sense that even though she didn't know exactly what the future held, she would be okay.

As the tents came into view, her breath caught at the sight of David sitting on the deck reading. His hair, tousled from sleep, was uncombed but gave him a rugged look, along with the day-old beard on his face. Since he'd returned from fighting the fires, she'd come to realise how much she truly loved him and what a fool she'd been for leaving him dangling for so long. She could have easily lost him. He looked up and she lifted her hand and smiled. He set his book down, and after taking the stairs in one big stride, loped towards her wearing a grin that sent her pulse racing. Reaching her, he bundled her in his arms, lowered his mouth and kissed her gently but passionately. "Good morning, my love," he whispered between kisses.

Drawing back, she gazed into his eyes and smiled. "And good morning to you."

He had breakfast already prepared—a fresh fruit platter, yoghurt, and croissants. "I didn't think you'd want bacon and eggs."

"You know what," she said, selecting a plump, juicy looking strawberry from the bowl and popping it into her mouth, "I'm actually ravenous, and I think I could eat a whole pig."

His brows lifted. "Really?"

She grinned as she nodded. "I think the sickness has gone."

"That's great news, because fruit and yoghurt don't really do it for me."

"I know that. But it was really sweet of you."

"Thank you for saying so."

"You're welcome," she said as she sat on the chair opposite him and poured juice into two glasses and handed him one. Easing back in the chair to take in the peaceful, bushland setting, a rustling in the undergrowth caught her attention. Leaning forward, she spotted a large goanna waddling along and pointed it out to David. "You don't see that every day in the city."

"No, you don't. It's magical out here, isn't it?"

"It sure is," she agreed.

"And this tent beats ours hands down."

"Yes, but you can't put it in the back of the car." She chuckled as she chose another strawberry and slid it into her mouth.

"You do have a point." Leaning forward, he took her hand and gently rubbed her skin with his thumb. "I wouldn't mind going camping again one day. It seems so long since we went anywhere."

"Did you forget we're camping out tonight?" she asked, angling her head.

"No, and I'm looking forward to it."

She smiled. "So am I." Just then, her phone rang.

∽

DAVID STUDIED Serena's face as she took the call. She'd

mouthed that it was Danny, and as he realised with great clarity that the answer he'd been seeking for so long was about to be revealed, his heart raced and his palms grew sweaty. Although he knew that nothing could bring his mother and siblings back, and that God could release him from his feelings of guilt, he was still anxious to know the truth. *Was he responsible for the fire?*

Serena's facial expressions were difficult to read. In fact, she turned her head so he couldn't see her properly, which didn't bode well, and her responses were ambiguous. She was trying to soften the blow, of that he was sure. She wasn't saying much, and his mind was swirling.

But when she ended the call and faced him, her eyes sparkled and she said words he could barely believe. "You didn't light the fire, David."

Relief washed over him as tears stung his eyes. "Are you sure?" he whispered.

She nodded. "Danny found a report that confirmed it was an accident. Your father had been drinking and your parents had an argument. He stormed out of the house, taking you with him. In the process, it seems he knocked over a candle, but your mother had taken to her room with the younger children and didn't realise the house was on fire until it was too late."

Tears streamed down his cheeks. "I can't believe it."

She eased herself onto his lap, and cradled his head in her arms.

His breathing calmed as he leaned his head against her chest, her warmth comforting him. "I should have done the research myself, but I was too scared of what I'd find."

"It's okay. We're all fearful of things at times. Just look at me. I was so fearful of even going outside, but I've come to see that God doesn't expect us to be super-human. He simply wants us to be honest and open and to leave the rest to Him."

"I think it's going to take time to sink in, but I already feel a weight has lifted from me."

She kissed the top of his head. "I'm so glad. Now, where's that bacon and eggs? If we're going riding, I need sustenance."

He smiled. "Coming right up." Setting her on the floor, he rubbed her forearms and gazed into her eyes. "Serena, thank you for finding out. Knowing I wasn't responsible is going to make all the difference in the world to me."

Her mouth twitched with a smile as she leaned in and brushed her lips gently across his. "You're more than welcome."

CHAPTER 28

Seated around the campfire that night, leaning against Frank under a star-studded sky, Maggie counted her blessings. The day's ride had been entertaining to say the least. Although she now lived on a cattle station, she realised she knew very little about the cattle raised on Goddard Downs. For the drive, Josh and Sean had selected twenty Brahman crosses they thought would be well behaved, but they were anything but. She and Serena had hung back as the men, including Frank and David, tried to keep them in line, and several times the women had laughed with hysterics as the cattle outsmarted them.

But it was such a great experience, and spending time with Serena was special. Serena told her she wasn't sure what she would do about work. Having received a large insurance payout, she didn't need to go back, but she needed to be doing something to fill her time until the baby was born. She wasn't overly eager to take the talk-back host job Danny had offered her, but now that she was coming to terms with her permanent scarring, she was thinking about the possibility of doing some kind of motivational speaking, similar to Turia Pitt. When Serena told her that, Maggie had struggled to contain her joy. How far she'd come in such little time was nothing short of a miracle.

And now, seated around the fire, listening to her and David chat about God and how amazing creation was, Maggie's heart was truly blessed. She tilted her head to Frank and squeezed his arm. "This is wonderful. I wish we could do it more often."

He kissed the top of her head. "I think we could arrange it quite easily."

"Good. Although I'm not sure about the cattle part of it."

"They add to the fun, my love."

She chuckled as she thought about some of the camera shots she'd taken today. "I guess they do. And you know, I think tourists will enjoy the experience, even though I still think we should consider expanding."

"Shh. Enough of that. I had a call from Rafi Tamala this morning while we were getting the cattle ready. He's interested in buying our processed beef, and he wants to come for a visit."

Straightening, Maggie stared at him. "And when were you going to tell me that?"

He shrugged. "It slipped my mind. Sorry."

"How could it slip your mind? That's amazing, Frank!"

"Yes. It could be the answer to our prayers."

"It certainly could be. God's been good to us, hasn't He?"

"He sure has. We should never doubt His providence."

She chuckled. "I've been learning that lesson."

When he pulled her closer, she snuggled against him. "If I go to sleep, you'll need to carry me to the swag."

He kissed her forehead. "That will be my pleasure."

But she didn't fall asleep there, because Josh pulled out a ukulele and began singing campfire songs. Sean made a damper with David and Serena's help, and after cooking it in the coals, they all enjoyed the delicious campfire bread with oodles of butter and mugs of billy tea. Frank finished the evening with a word of prayer, a fitting end to a wonderful day.

Morning came way too soon. The swag was more comfortable than Maggie had expected and she could have stayed there longer except for the sun streaming down on her. Crawling out of the swag, she stretched and looked around. Frank was seated beside the fire with Josh and Sean, cooking breakfast, while David and Serena were still asleep in their separate swags. She didn't know how they could still be asleep because the kookaburras were so loud, plus, the tantalising aroma of sizzling sausages and bacon wafted in the air.

She walked over to Frank and placed her hand on his shoulder. "Good morning, my love. It smells good."

"It does, doesn't it. Would you like a cup of tea?"

"I'd love one, thanks. It's a gorgeous morning, isn't it?" Rubbing her hands together, she lifted her face to the sun.

"It is." He took the billy off the grate and poured a mug of steaming tea.

"Thank you," she said gratefully as she took it and sat on a log beside him. "Did the cattle behave last night?"

"Nope," Josh replied. "We'll have to round them up this morning before we head off."

"I think you should have a crack at it, my love," Frank said, grinning.

"Me?"

"Yes, you."

"I wouldn't be any good. They'd probably run from me."

"You'll never know until you try."

Remembering her attempt at fencing, she thought that perhaps he was right. Until you actually tried something, you never knew what you were capable of. "Okay, I'll give it a go, but you have to promise you won't laugh at me."

"I don't think I can promise that, but I'm sure you'll be fine." He reached out and grabbed her hand and gave a smile filled with confidence.

Serena and David finally emerged from their swags and joined the group, and while they ate breakfast around the fire, Maggie convinced Serena to also have a go at rounding the cattle.

∼

A LITTLE WHILE LATER, as Frank watched Maggie trying her best to outsmart one of the brahman crosses and get it to join the others, he chuckled to himself. It was sure entertaining, but she seemed to be enjoying herself. For a city gal, she'd taken to station life like a fish to water, and he didn't think he could love her any more than he did right now. God had truly blessed their marriage, and he was so looking forward to having her beside him in the years to come. Whatever their future held, they would face it together.

When Maggie finally succeeded, the grin on her face was as

broad as they came. Her eyes were bright as she joined him at the back of the mob. "I did it!"

"You sure did. I'm so proud of you, Maggie. You looked like a pro out there."

She laughed. "You're such a liar, Frank Goddard!"

"Nope. It's the truth. I reckon we could make a ringer out of you yet."

"I think I'll stick to the veggie patch if you don't mind. But I have to admit, this was fun."

"And there's still plenty to come. I hope you've got your dancing shoes ready for tomorrow night."

She laughed again. "I sure do."

CHAPTER 29

The neighbours began arriving at three in the afternoon. Doug and Maryann McMurtrie arrived first by helicopter with their two children, Stuart and Sally, followed soon after by Trevor and Barbara Hanlon and their four children, Trudie, Michael, Simon and Sophie.

The latter had arrived by road since the river between the two stations was now crossable for high range vehicles. The two families set up camp in a paddock Frank and the boys had cleared and were soon joined by another family, the Clermonts, Brady, Sue, and their three children, Natalie, Brodie and Penny. The last to arrive were Robert and Maria Thomson, the current owners of Brampton Downs where Maggie and Frank had married.

The paddock resembled a campground by the time they were all set up, especially since the crew from Goddard Downs had also decided to camp out. It had been such a long time since they'd all been together in one place, and Frank took pride in introducing Maggie, Serena and David to his neighbours.

Olivia, Janella and Maggie had prepared a wonderful but simple spread that was served throughout the afternoon and evening, while the boys barbecued Goddard Downs steaks and sausages.

The children, ranging in age from four to eighteen, although initially shy with each other, finally broke through their shyness and played together in the paddock all afternoon.

After everyone finished eating, Frank stood and cleared his throat. It took several moments for the adults to call the children in and for everyone to quieten, but when they did, he smiled at the group gathered around. A motley crew, not merely neighbours, but friends.

"I'd like to thank you all for coming today. It's great to see everyone gathered together like this. It's been too long since the last time. Most of us have been struggling to stay afloat this past year, and we've been working hard and not taking enough time to relax and be neighbourly.

"I don't know what the future holds, but I have confidence we'll all survive as we embrace new opportunities that come our way. I know you're not all praying people, but I'd like to pray a blessing over us and our families. As you know, Goddard Downs has been in the Goddard family for four generations, and I know for a fact that if it wasn't for God's mercy and providence, I wouldn't be standing here today with my beautiful wife, Maggie." He waved her over and as she joined him, she slipped her hand into his and gave him a warm smile. "I'd like to give God the glory and commit our future to Him. Will you join me?"

The group nodded and bowed their heads as he prayed. "Dear Lord, we thank You for Your many blessings. We also thank You for times of trial and challenge when we're forced to reassess our priorities and look outside ourselves. Help us to always be ethical in our dealings and to not be lured by the offer of a quick dollar. Bless our families, dear Lord, and may we each know the amazing, abiding love of the Saviour, in whose name we pray. Amen."

Following a chorus of amens, Frank said, "Now, let the party begin!" He gave a nod to Janella who turned the portable sound system up. "Take your partners for a good old-fashioned barn dance!" Hooking his arm around Maggie's waist, he skilfully two-stepped her into the cleared area.

She laughed as she followed his lead. "So, now I get to see you boogie!"

"You sure do, darlin'." He twirled her around and pulled her tight, planting a kiss on her lips.

They danced for hours, and by the time midnight came, everyone was more than ready for bed. The camp grew quiet as one by one, everyone settled in their tents for the night.

Frank snuggled close to Maggie after sliding into their swag. "Well, my love, did you enjoy your first shindig?"

"I loved it. We'll have to do it more often. But you know what warmed my heart the most?"

"No, tell me."

"Serena enjoying herself. She looked the happiest I've ever seen her."

"They're going to be all right, you know that, don't you?"

She nodded. "Yes, I do. I can't imagine her with a baby, but I'm sure she'll be a great mother."

"And David will be a wonderful father."

"I wonder when he'll pop the question again?"

"When he's good and ready, my love. No need for any meddling by you."

"Frank! As if I'd ever meddle!"

He chuckled and stroked her cheek with the tip of his finger, her lips so close he could smell the hint of the hot chocolate they'd drunk for supper. "I love you, Maggie," he said as he brushed those lips with his own.

"I love you, too, Frank." Her whisper filled his heart with joy and his body with need. He wove his fingers through her hair and pressed his lips harder to hers.

∽

Maggie had no need to meddle. The following morning, Serena and David joined them for breakfast, and from the grins on their faces, she knew something was going on. When they announced their engagement, Maggie jumped up and threw her arms around them both. "Congratulations! I'm so happy for you!"

"Thank you," they both replied.

Of course, Maggie wanted to know the details of the proposal, so as they sipped tea around the fire, Serena told her that David had suggested they take a walk while everyone was enjoying supper and chatting together. "I had no idea what he had in mind, but he led me to the lookout not far from here, and in the light of the full moon, he got down on one knee and asked me to marry him. He even gave me a ring. It was the most romantic moment ever, and this time I said yes."

Maggie admired her beautiful ring. "I'm so excited for you, sweetheart. I know God has good things in store for you both. It might have been a slow path, but you got there in the end."

Serena smiled. "Yes, there were certainly some twists and turns, but we both have peace about the future."

"And I couldn't be happier for you." She pulled Serena close and hugged her. "God bless you, my darling girl."

"Thank you, Mum. And you can stop crying now."

"I'm not crying!"

"Yes you are. And you're making me cry, too."

"We're a good pair, aren't we?"

Serena chuckled. "Yes. Who would have thought?"

EPILOGUE

Two months later, Maggie and Frank arrived in Darwin on a sunny afternoon in early May for Serena and David's wedding. They drove the whole way since the rains had stopped and the rivers were now crossable, which meant that tourists had begun flocking into the top end. A number had already been guests in the eco tents and others had enjoyed the overnight cattle drive experience, and the bookings for both looked promising for the season. As a result, the rest of Frank's family couldn't leave the station to attend the wedding.

Maggie was glad he seemed happy enough to hand over the reins for the next six weeks, at least, to Julian. After the wedding, they were flying to be guests at Rafi Tamala's home in the hills outside of Medan in Northern Sumatra. Rafi's recent visit to Goddard Downs had gone so well that he'd extended the invitation to them before he left. He'd also said he would draw up an agreement to purchase one-hundred head of processed beef each month. Frank was ecstatic and relieved by the news, although rumours were floating that the ban on live exports might soon be lifted.

Either way, they were in a good position, since having accepted Maggie's offer of financial assistance, Goddard Downs could now satisfy all regulatory requirements without the need to borrow money from the bank or be tempted to bend the rules. Not that Frank would ever have done that. In fact, on the night of the shindig, he'd told her he'd had a chat with several of the other men and discovered that they, too, had been leaned on by Officer Shepherd for a bribe, and they'd agreed the authorities needed to be alerted to his illegal and unethical practices. The investigation was well underway, and Officer Shepherd had been stood down pending the outcome.

While in Darwin, they were staying in Maggie's apartment, which had been standing empty since before their own wedding. While there, she was planning on deciding what to do with it since it seemed wasteful to have it sitting empty for so long. Frank had suggested renting it out, but she was almost at the point of deciding to sell, so he didn't push.

Opening the door and walking inside felt strange and, in fact, it was almost like walking into somebody else's home. It didn't take Maggie long to make her decision. While they were seated on the balcony having a cool drink, she told Frank she'd sell it. "As lovely as this view is over the bay, Goddard Downs is now my home."

He smiled and took her hand. "I'm so glad to hear you say that. Not that I don't like it here, but it's so—"

"Confining." She grinned as she cut him off. "I know. You're a country boy, Frank Goddard, and we have no need of a city apartment. We have plenty of family we can stay with whenever we're in town."

"We sure do. And I somehow expect you're going to be visiting often with a new grandchild on the way."

"You're probably right. But anyway, what shall we do tonight?"

"I was thinking we could have an early dinner at Pearls, followed by a stroll along the boardwalk for old-time's sake."

"That sounds perfect to me." She leaned in and kissed him.

∼

ON THE DAY of the wedding, David couldn't wipe the grin off his face. When he'd proposed to Serena the second time, he'd prayed she'd say yes and was ecstatic when she did. They agreed to not wait long to get married, especially with the baby on the way. Serena was already showing, and besides, they longed to be living together again. She'd kept living with Jeremy and Emma, but she was more than ready to move back into her own place.

Troy had stayed with him overnight, and they'd had a bit of a boys' night with pizza and a few beers. Not that he drank much these days, but it was hard not to enjoy a beer every now and again in this hot climate. He thanked Troy for giving him the book that had literally opened his eyes to who Jesus was. Since then, he hadn't looked back and had been eager to grow in his newfound faith, and he quickly realised that the sense of belonging he'd been seeking for so long had now been found. He was a child of the King. He'd always feel sad about what happened to his family, but he felt grateful that he'd been raised by loving relatives, and now he was blessed with a new family. The Goddards. He'd left Goddard Downs with an open invitation to return whenever he wanted. "There'll always be a job for you here," Josh had told him not long before they left. He wasn't sure what Serena would think about living out there, and he wouldn't even consider it if she wasn't fully onboard, but the idea niggled at the back of his mind. He'd pray about it and see what eventuated.

The day was glorious, which was perfect, because they'd planned an outdoor ceremony at East Point, overlooking the blue waters of Fanny Bay. He'd wanted a morning wedding, mainly because he thought he'd go stir crazy waiting for the afternoon to come, but she wanted a late afternoon wedding because the light was better for photos. He honestly didn't care about photos, but they seemed important to her, and considering how she hadn't even wanted to go outside a few months earlier, he had to support her.

Troy had suggested they play a round of golf in the morning, and he'd also invited Frank and Jeremy since the girls were doing their own thing. A champagne breakfast apparently, but not real champagne, Serena had assured him. It was the pretend stuff that still tasted okay, followed by a session with the hairdresser and make-up artist. Serena had engaged the same hairdresser who'd given her all the tips that day when her hair was coloured pink. She'd assured David she wouldn't do that again, but he did wonder if she'd walk down the aisle with a different colour. He wouldn't put it past her, but he didn't care. He simply wanted to marry her.

The time finally came to get ready. He and Troy were wearing lightweight cream suits with white shirts. It didn't take them long to dress, and soon Troy was driving them to the point. They'd kept the wedding party small since neither had seen the need for a lot of attendants. Troy was his best man and Emma was Serena's maid of honour. Jeremy would walk with her since Cliff was still in the hospital and not attending the wedding. Word was that he could be in there for a long time to come.

When they arrived at the point, a number of guests were already there. Some of his work buddies and their partners, some of Serena's work colleagues, including Danny, whom David had already thanked for gathering the information about the fire, Aunt Heather and Uncle Gordon who'd raised him, Auntie Peg and his cousins, and Frank and Maggie. He and Troy greeted everyone and then David spoke briefly to John, the officiating pastor. John was the pastor at Jeremy and Emma's church that he and Serena had also been attending. The only people missing were Serena, Emma, Jeremy, and Sebastian, who was excited to be the page boy.

A hush grew amongst the guests as the bridal car approached and stopped. Jeremy was the first to get out, looking dapper in a dark suit, followed by Sebastian who looked very cute in his matching but much smaller suit. And then Emma emerged, breathtaking in a pastel pink gown.

But David had eyes only for Serena. As she stepped out of the stretch limo, his breath caught. She was wearing a snugly fitting white gown that showed off her baby bump for all to see. A veil covered her face and her scars. Not that they bothered him—he didn't see them anymore. Through the veil he could see her hair was a deep brown, almost black. Her natural colour. He smiled as he caught her eye. He wouldn't have cared if it had been blue, pink, purple, or red, but her natural colour was perfect.

She linked her arm through Jeremy's and they followed Sebastian and Emma on a slow walk towards him. His heart nearly burst when she reached him and Jeremy placed her hand in his and they shared a smile.

Pastor John began the ceremony and although he did his best to listen, David was waiting for the moment when they would be declared man and wife. It finally came, and then, when the pastor said he could now kiss his bride, David faced her and slowly lifted her veil and gazed into her eyes. His heart beat a crescendo as he lowered his face and their lips met. He longed to kiss her passionately, but the time for that would come soon, so for now, he simply pressed his lips against hers and whispered words of love.

∽

Serena smiled at her new husband with happy tears in her eyes. The ceremony had been perfect, and she felt so very blessed to now be introduced as Mr. and Mrs. David and Serena Kramer. She couldn't wait to be alone with him. It seemed an eternity since he'd proposed, although it had only been two months, but she longed to be a family as they eagerly looked forward to the arrival of their baby.

Their photos were taken as the sun set slowly over Fanny Bay, followed with the reception at the Yacht Club function rooms. It was a fun evening, the food was great, the speeches were passable. David brought tears to her eyes and a lump to her throat as he spoke about the journey they'd been on to get to this point and how God had so graciously drawn them to Himself and given them both peace.

They'd danced for a bit and cut the cake, but when he whispered in her ear it was time to go, she was more than ready. They hugged and kissed everyone goodbye, leaving her mum and Frank until last. Her mum had tears in her eyes as they hugged, and Serena told her to stop it. "You're going to ruin your make-up."

Her mum laughed. "I think it's too late for that."

She kissed her mum's cheek and then smiled. "Thanks for believing in me, Mum. You're the best mother any girl could ever want."

∼

As Serena and David drove away, Maggie's heart soared despite the tears that didn't want to stop. She waved until the car was out of sight, and then Frank turned her to face him, nudging her chin with his thumb. "Let's dry those tears and get out of here."

"And where are we going?"

"Hmmm… let me see… I know of an apartment that overlooks the bay that may have champagne, chocolates and a big comfy queen-sized bed."

She grinned. "That sounds like the perfect place to spend the night."

Leaning in, he lowered his mouth and kissed her tenderly.

Be anxious for nothing, *but in everything by prayer and supplica-*

tion, with thanksgiving, let your requests be made known to God; and the peace of God, which surpasses all understanding, will guard your hearts and minds through Christ Jesus. Philippians 4:6-7

NOTE FROM THE AUTHOR

I hope you enjoyed "Slow Path to Peace", and that perhaps in some small way it helped you cope better with these troubling times we're experiencing now.

Frank and Maggie's' story continues in "Slow Ride Home". Reserve your copy now so you don't miss it!

To make sure you don't miss any of my new releases, why not join my Readers' list? http://www.julietteduncan.com/linkspage/282748 You'll also receive a free thank-you copy of "Hank and Sarah - A Love Story", a clean love story with God at the center.

Enjoyed "Slow Path to Peace"? You can make a big difference. Help other people find this book by writing a review and telling them why you liked it. Honest reviews of my books help bring them to the attention of other readers just like yourself, and I'd be very grateful if you could spare just five minutes to leave a review (it can be as short as you like) on the book's Amazon page.

Blessings and love,

Juliette

P.S. The book that Troy gave David to read is a book written by a friend of mine, Jason Elsmore, one of the pastors of a large Baptist church here in Brisbane. It's a very Aussie book, but if you're interested, you can check it out here: https://jesusthebloke.com.au/

P.P.S. Keep reading for a bonus chapter of "The Preacher's Son", releasing on July 21.

Chapter 1

As I sat on the beach with the sun warming my back while Hayden taught the kids to surf, I reflected on how blessed we were. Despite feeling a strange kind of restlessness over the past few months, which I simply put down to the fact that we were getting older—a touch of mid-thirties angst, I certainly had nothing to be unhappy about. Life couldn't be more perfect.

Hayden and I had been married nearly ten years and had been blessed with two beautiful children. Elijah had come first after a fraught couple of years of trying, followed swiftly by Rosie. Motherhood was hard work, but also far more rewarding than I ever could have expected. Of course, the fact that Hayden was so hands-on with the children made things so much easier.

In that sense, I guessed we had a less than traditional marriage. Hayden worked part-time in construction, which meant I was able to pursue a full-time career as a successful defence attorney. Outside of my family and church, my career was my pride and my passion. Every so often a pang of guilt besieged me when I thought about what Hayden had given up for me, but he seemed happy enough and had never said otherwise.

I had no idea, that evening at the beach, that everything was about to change so drastically.

Our life had fallen into a comfortable rhythm of work, family time (more often than not spent at the beach) and church. We also volunteered one evening a week at the local homeless shelter. We'd started one Christmas when the children were babies, purely to help out because numbers were low, and had enjoyed it so much we were still there. If enjoyed was the right word. It was heartbreaking to see the rough hand life could deal people, but it was also uplifting to realise the difference a smile and a kind word could make.

Hayden loved being of service to others, so much so that every now and then he tentatively suggested we go on a mission holiday. Whenever he did, I simply nodded and smiled, but secretly hoped the idea would be forgotten. Such a drastic change of scenery, so far out of my comfort zone, left me cold. Although I dealt with tough cases every day in court, I knew what I was doing there. I was a competent lawyer. A mission trip would be something else entirely.

Yet, I often had the niggling feeling that it was simply a matter of time before Hayden would want to fulfil that side of him, and although he never mentioned it, I'd never forgotten that he'd walked out of Theological College to be with me, breaking his father's heart in the process.

My grandmother, as my mother still often reminded me, had warned me never to kiss a preacher's son. Only later did I find out the sad story that lay behind her warnings. That my grandmother's preacher's son had cheated on her and left her heartbroken. When I had indeed kissed a preacher's son—Hayden and he then left me to go off for ministry training, I wished I'd listened to her.

But then he came back, and here we were, ten years later, with all the blessings we could ever ask for.

It was because of Hayden that I'd found my own faith, and I said a silent prayer of gratitude as Elijah and Rosie ran up the beach towards me, their child-sized surfboards tucked under their arms. Hayden followed, looking exhausted but grinning widely. He was still such a handsome man, deeply tanned from working outside in the summer sun, and at times like this my breath still caught in my throat simply looking at him. Not for the first time did I think that we really had to start making more time for each other as a couple and not just as parents. It was an easy trap to fall into.

"You should have come back in, Pen. The water's terrific."

"So is the sun." I laughed, holding my face to it. "I wanted to soak some of it up. You guys looked like you were having plenty of fun."

"I'm a better surfer than Elijah," five-year-old Rosie said. "I didn't fall in as many times as he did."

"That's because Daddy was holding you!" six-year-old Elijah protested.

Rosie pouted and I laughed as I got to my feet. The kids adored each other, but they were too close in age as siblings not to bicker constantly.

"Stop fighting, you both did great," Hayden admonished, winking at me. We walked back up the beach together as the evening sun started to spread across the sky.

We grabbed some fish and chips from our favourite take-away shop and sat at a table overlooking the ocean to eat them. When we reached home, we took it in turns to bath the kids and put them to bed. I was just coming out of Elijah's room, having finally gotten him to sleep after no less than three bedtime stories, when I heard Hayden talking on the phone in the landing. It would be his parents. He usually phoned them every few weeks, typically on a Saturday. I was carrying on into our own bedroom to fold laundry when something in his tone made me stop.

"No, I haven't forgotten, Dad. But I can't see it happening now, not with the kids so young and with Penny's job..."

Was his father talking to him about ministry again? Hayden's father had always wanted him to follow in his footsteps and be a pastor, too. Although he'd given us his blessing all those years ago and was a devoted grandfather, I was always aware, no matter how many years passed, of an underlying disappointment. And although he'd never said such a thing, I always wondered if he didn't blame me for distracting Hayden from his destiny...or the destiny his father wanted for him, anyway. If he wouldn't have been happier if his only son had married a more traditional wife, without such a demanding career.

Because although I had ignored my grandmother's instructions to never kiss a preacher's son, I was certain that I didn't ever want to be a preacher's wife. I saw the way Hayden's mother had taken a back seat to his father's pastoral responsibilities, playing the role of pastor's wife perfectly, and I knew that I would be terrible at it. My faith in God had grown and blossomed over the years...but a life devoted to my husband's career in the church? That could never be me.

Of course, even as I thought the words, an inner voice reminded me that Hayden had sacrificed for *my* career. I was pretty sure he'd never planned on being a lawyer's husband, either.

I hurried into the bedroom and shut the door behind me so that I couldn't be tempted to eavesdrop any further and got on with the laundry, trying not to wonder what was being said. When Hayden walked into the bedroom, I smiled at him, trying not to let my thoughts show.

"Elijah's finally asleep too. I'm going to fold these and iron the kids' outfits for church in the morning, then maybe we could cuddle up and watch a movie together?" It had been a long time since we'd done that, most weekend evenings I went to bed early with a good novel. In the week I was always exhausted from work.

"That sounds nice, but no rom coms?"

"Only if you promise no superhero movies," I said with a grin.

Hayden raised an eyebrow. "That doesn't leave us with a lot."

It didn't. We compromised on a historical drama we hadn't seen before, but it was terrible and we were both yawning before the movie was halfway through. Laughing, we went to bed for an early night after all.

But I couldn't shake the gnawing feeling in my gut about the phone call, and when Hayden pulled me into his arms for a cuddle after we'd gotten into bed, I blurted out before I was even aware that I was about to do so, "What was your father saying on the phone earlier tonight? You sounded serious."

In the half-light I was sure I saw Hayden flinch. *Was that a look of guilt on his face?*

"Just the usual," he said lightly. "Moaning about Mum's cooking."

His mother's culinary escapades were legendary, but for once I didn't laugh. "I heard you say something about not forgetting, but it was too late now. I wondered if he'd brought up wanting you to go into ministry again?"

There was a brief and loaded silence. Hayden's earlier plans to be a minister hadn't been mentioned between us for a long time. It was only in that moment that I realised how close to the surface the topic still bubbled.

"He did mention it...he was just reminding me there was still time."

I stared at him, watching the shadows fall on his face, and I was sure I was seeing sadness in his eyes. "Hayden," I said softly as I leaned on my elbow and voiced something I'd asked myself many times over the years, "Do you ever regret it?"

His eyes opened wide. "Leaving college to be with you? Of course not! I love our life, Pen. I love you. God sent me a sign, remember?" He kissed my forehead and I smiled as I did indeed remember. Hayden had gone to college even though we'd already fallen in love and he felt deeply conflicted, only to receive some unexpected advice from a wise stranger in the canteen, a stranger who had never been seen in the college before or since. Hayden was certain he'd been visited by an angel and had decided to follow his heart. I didn't know if I believed in angel visitations, but whatever happened that day, I thanked God for it, because it had brought Hayden back to me.

"I do remember," I whispered as I straightened and took his

hand and drew circles on it. "It's just sometimes I worry that construction isn't going to be enough for you, not forever, or once the kids get older. You were brought up expecting to follow in your father's footsteps."

"I was," he said with a sigh, "and I thought my path was all mapped out for me. But God had other plans. I enjoy my job, Penny, and I love how much time I get to be a father. Some men miss out on that."

I nodded, even as I felt the usual twinge of mother-guilt that I worked long hours myself. I took extended maternity leave with the both, and had really felt the lack of that time with them when I went back to work. I wondered if that was the source of my restlessness.

I should have left the subject alone instead of picking at it like a wound that needed more time to heal, but suddenly I needed to know the answer. "But be honest," I pressed. "If I was prepared to work less hours so that you could go for ministry training, would you want to go?"

When he didn't immediately answer, my heart sank a little.

"I don't know," he finally said. "That's my honest answer. My dad was always so convinced that some kind of career in the church was my destiny, that I suppose that sunk in. I do wonder sometimes what it would have been like. But I can't tell you if I would want to do it now. Maybe...but I can't see you as a pastor's wife." He chuckled and I knew he was joking and trying to lighten the mood, but his words were so close to echoing my thoughts just a few minutes before that I couldn't laugh.

Hayden stroked my face and his touch soothed me as it always did. "Penny, I love you," he murmured, gazing into my eyes. "That's the one thing I know for certain. God knows the right path."

But what if God's path wasn't the same as *my* path? What if I really was holding Hayden back? I didn't like the uncertainty that was suddenly filling me.

"What is it?" Hayden asked.

I shook my head, not even understanding myself what I was feeling. "I don't know. I've been feeling weirdly restless lately. A little more anxious than usual. I don't know why, because life is wonderful."

I expected Hayden to look surprised or even concerned, but instead he nodded as though he understood. "Funnily enough, so have I. Just the last few months or so, it's as if things are ripe for a change. But then I feel I'm being ungrateful when we've been given so much. I figured it was just some pre-midlife crisis." He laughed, and I laughed with him, but the uneasiness didn't go away.

We kissed lightly and then Hayden fell asleep while I lay awake, staring into the dark. I tried to tell myself that I was being silly, allowing myself to get caught up in worries that didn't need to be worried about, but I couldn't convince myself. It felt as though something was significant about his father bringing up that old but never forgotten subject, just as both of us admitting to feeling a little complacent about life.

I prayed, asking God for peace of mind, and immediately felt soothed, if not entirely at peace. I wished I could be more like Hayden, who was easier going than me and had no trouble placing his life in God's hands.

Help me do Your will, Lord, I prayed silently. But as I settled down into the pillow, I couldn't help wondering, *what if it was God's will for me to become a preacher's wife after all?*

∼

TO KEEP READING Penny and Hayden's story, reserve your copy of *"The Preacher's Son"* here. It's due to release on July 21. Penny and Hayden's story starts in the novella, *"Never Kiss a Preacher's Son"* which is one of the 21 sweet romance stories contained in the Sweet Kisses Boxset which also releases on July 21. Reserve your copy of this amazing set now for just 99c, but don't forget to pre-order your copy of *"Slow Ride Home"* at the same time!

OTHER BOOKS BY JULIETTE DUNCAN

Find all of Juliette Duncan's books on her website:
www.julietteduncan.com/library

A Sunburned Land

Slow Road to Love

A divorced reporter on a remote assignment. An alluring cattleman who captures her heart…

Slow Journey to Joy

An emergency dash to Paris, an engagement on hold, and an ex-husband who wants her back…

Slow Path to Peace

With their lives are stripped bare, can Serena and David find peace?

Slow Ride Home

He's a cowboy who lives his life with abandon. She's spirited and fiercely independent…

Transformed by Love Christian Romance Series

Book 1 - *Because We Loved*

A decorated Lieutenant Colonel plagued with guilt. A captivating widow whose husband was killed under his watch...

Book 2 - *Because We Forgave*

A fallen TV personality hiding from his failures. An ex-wife and family facing their fears...

Book 3 - *Because We Dreamed*

When dreams are shattered, can hope be restored?

Book 4 - *Because We Believed*

A single mom forging a new life. A handsome chaplain who steals her heart...

Billionaires with Heart Christian Romance Series

Her Kind-Hearted Billionaire

A reluctant billionaire, a grieving young woman, and the trip that changes their lives forever...

Her Generous Billionaire

A grieving billionaire, a solo mother, and a woman determined to

sabotage their relationship...

Her Disgraced Billionaire

A billionaire in jail, a nurse who cares, and the challenge that changes their lives forever...

Her Compassionate Billionaire

A widowed billionaire with three young children. A replacement nanny who helps change his life...

"The Billionaires with Heart Christian Romance Series" is a series of stand-alone books that are both God honoring and entertaining. Get your copy now,

enjoy and be blessed!

A Time for Everything Series

A Time For Everything Series is a mature-age contemporary Christian romance series set in Sydney, Australia and Texas, USA. If you like real-life characters, faith-filled families, and friendships that become something more, then you'll love these inspirational second-chance romances.

The True Love Series

Set in Australia, what starts out as simple love story grows into a family saga, including a dad battling bouts of depression and guilt, an ex-wife with issues of her own, and a young step-mum trying to mother a teenager who's confused and hurting. Through it all, a love story is woven. A love story between a caring God and His precious children as He gently draws them to Himself and walks with them through the trials and joys of life.

"A beautiful Christian story. I enjoyed all of the books in this series. They all brought out Christian concepts of faith in action."

"Wonderful set of books. Weaving the books from story to story. Family living, God, & learning to trust Him with all their hearts."

The Precious Love Series

The Precious Love Series continues the story of Ben, Tessa and Jayden from the The True Love Series, although each book can be read on its own. All of the books in this series will warm your heart and draw you closer to the God who loves and cherishes you without condition.

"I loved all the books by Juliette, but those about Jaydon and Angie's stories are my favorites...can't wait for the next one..."

"Juliette Duncan has earned my highest respect as a Christian romance writer. She continues to write such touching stories about real life and the tragedies, turmoils, and joys that happen while we are living. The words that she uses to write about her characters relationships with God can only come from someone that has had a very close & special with her Lord and Savior herself. I have read all of her books and if you are a reader of Christian fiction books I would highly recommend her books." Vicki

The Shadows Series

An inspirational romance, a story of passion and love, and of God's inexplicable desire to free people from pasts that haunt them so they can live a life full of His peace, love and forgiveness, regardless of the circumstances. Book 1, *"Lingering Shadows"* is set in England, and follows the story of Lizzy, a headstrong, impulsive young lady from a privileged background, and Daniel, a roguish Irishman who sweeps her off her feet. But can Lizzy leave the shadows of her past behind and give Daniel the love he deserves, and will Daniel find freedom and release in God?

Hank and Sarah - A Love Story, *the Prequel to "The Madeleine*

Richards Series" is a FREE thank you gift for joining my mailing list. You'll also be the first to hear about my next books and get exclusive sneak previews. Get your free copy at www.julietteduncan.com/subscribe

The Madeleine Richards Series

Although the 3 book series is intended mainly for pre-teen/ Middle Grade girls, it's been read and enjoyed by people of all ages.

"Juliette has a fabulous way of bringing her characters to life. Maddy is at typical teenager with authentic views and actions that truly make it feel like you are feeling her pain and angst. You want to enter into her situation and make everything better. Mom and soon to be dad respond to her with love and gentle persuasion while maintaining their faith and trust in Jesus, whom they know, will give them wisdom as they continue on their lives journey. Appropriate for teenage readers but any age can enjoy." Amazon Reader

The Potter's House Books...stories of hope, redemption, and second chances. Find out more here:

http://pottershousebooks.com/our-books/

The Homecoming

Can she surrender a life of fame and fortune to find true love?

Unchained

Imprisoned by greed – redeemed by love

Blessings of Love

She's going on mission to help others. He's going to win her heart.

The Hope We Share

Can the Master Potter work in Rachel and Andrew's hearts and give them a second chance at love?

When Love Abounds

Can the Master Potter work in Megan's heart and save her marriage?

Stand Alone Christian Romantic Suspense

Leave Before He Kills You

When his face grew angry, I knew he could murder…

ABOUT THE AUTHOR

Juliette Duncan is a Christian fiction author, passionate about writing stories that will touch her readers' hearts and make a difference in their lives. Although a trained school teacher, Juliette spent many years working alongside her husband in their own business, but is now relishing the opportunity to follow her passion for writing stories she herself would love to read. Based in Brisbane, Australia, Juliette and her husband have five adult children, eight grandchildren, and an elderly long haired dachshund. Apart from writing, Juliette loves exploring the great world we live in, and has travelled extensively, both within Australia and overseas. She also enjoys social dancing and eating out.

Connect with Juliette:

Email: author@julietteduncan.com

Website: www.julietteduncan.com

Facebook: www.facebook.com/JulietteDuncanAuthor

Twitter: https://twitter.com/Juliette_Duncan

Printed in Great Britain
by Amazon